CHAPTER 1

Hannah

Hannah woke with a throbbing headache that coincided with a sharp pain over her right eye. It had been another rough night and she would do everything she could to forget it. She wanted to stay in bed and avoid the day ahead, but she felt herself automatically reach for her mirror to assess the damage. Her right eye was blood shot and surrounded by a black bruise. It would lead to too many questions. She would have to give school a miss for the fifth time in two weeks. Thankfully it was Friday and she only had 3 classes.

Her teachers wouldn't miss her. In fact they'd be breathing a sigh of relief when there was no response to her name during roll call. The administration ladies would call, but they wouldn't be getting any answers. Just another unexplained absence. That was fine by Hannah. Because if people knew why she spent so many days at home, she would more than likely receive visits. Visits from people who could do more harm than good. Not that her mum and her pathetic boyfriend Dale didn't deserve to be put away, but where would that leave poor Chrissie? Besides, they both loved *her*. It was Hannah that was the problem. She wasn't Dale's daughter (thank god) and that somehow meant that Hannah was treated like an unwanted piece of rubbish. Her mother wasn't much better, not since Dale had come into the picture anyway. She had never been the greatest parent, but now she was nothing more than an associate. She didn't even try. And she really didn't care. Dale and Chrissie were number 1, while Hannah didn't even rank.

A loud knock on the door distracted Hannah from her thoughts. She instinctively grabbed for her doona and covered herself.

"Hannah? Are you ready for school?"

"Not going."

"What do you mean you're not going?"

Hannah rolled her eyes to herself. What did it matter? She wasn't going.

"I'm *not* going."

A slight pause.

"How is your sister supposed to get to school?"

Of course, her mum wasn't concerned about Hannah not going for her sake. By staying home she was unable to walk precious Chrissie.

"Not my problem. You take her."

"Hannah, you're her sister…"

"You're her fucking mum! You want her to get to school, you fucking take her!"

"Don't you speak to me like that," she opened the door before Hannah could stop her.

"Get out!" Hannah screamed. Forgetting the state of her face, she stood up and got out of bed, ready to yell at the top of her voice. Leanne simply starred at her daughter, not knowing what to do.

"Go on then, want to give me a black eye on the left to match?" said Hannah as the rush of blood to her head sent her a painful reminder.

Leanne said nothing. She simply backed out of the room, closed the door and left. '*World's best parent right there,*' thought Hannah.

She slumped back down on the bed, now more upset at her incompetent mother than the pain in her face. The bruising on her face would be no surprise to Leanne, who knew what went on yet did nothing to stop it. She had never seen the bruises this bad though, not this fresh and not this dark ; definitely never on the face. But would it shake Leanne to the point of ending it with Dale like she should have done 5 years ago? Of course not. Because she was weak, sad, lonely and 100% dependent on him. 100% dependent on a low life, abusive piece of scum. Nice.

Hannah grabbed some Panadol from under her bed and swallowed two, just enough to numb the pain. She planned on napping for the next 3 hours, by then her mum would probably be passed out drunk and she would be free to do as she pleased.

Hannah woke 4 hours later with her stomach rumbling. She wondered if she'd be able to share some mac and cheese with Chrissie, as there was no way Leanne would have taken her to school, so she would be home too. Hannah searched the house but there was no sign of Chrissie, her school bag was nowhere to be seen and her lunchbox remained on the kitchen table.

Hannah grabbed the last mac and cheese from the cupboard, when her mum appeared.

"Where's Chrissie?" demanded Hannah.

"At school, where do you think?"

"You mean you actually took her?"

"No, thanks to you, your sister walked by herself." "What?! You let her walk to school all by herself!?" "What do you mean *I* let her? You're the one who didn't go, you're the one who didn't take her!"

Hannah couldn't believe it. Well, actually she could. Her mother really was that useless. And so typical of her to blame Hannah. "She doesn't even have lunch! Not that she'll need it, she probably didn't even make it there!"

Her mum had apparently lost interest as she shrugged her shoulders and left. And this was supposedly the daughter she cared about.

Hannah had no choice but to pack Chrissie's lunch and take it to her. The only problem was there weren't many options to fill her lunch box. After scrounging around in the cupboard and fridge, Hannah could only find a worryingly brown banana and a slice of hard, stale bread. The rest was either out of date or would be too embarrassing to show up to her class with – even more so than the extra ripe banana and piece of bread. Hopefully one of the kids in her class would have something to share.

Hannah couldn't explain why she cared about her sister so much. Particularly when it was arguably her sister that had changed her life for the worse ever since she had come into it. Before Chrissie things were, well, different. Hannah definitely didn't swear at her mum and her mum definitely wouldn't have ignored a black eye. If Chrissie hadn't been born maybe Dale wouldn't be around either, and that could only be a good thing. Yet Hannah had an indescribable sense of protectiveness over her sister and a sense of care for her wellbeing.

As for Hannah's father, well, that was another story. He left before Hannah had even been born. Her mum barely spoke of him and when she did she described him as a 'Deadbeat' which Hannah always thought was a bit rich coming from her.

The way Hannah saw it, he had to be an improvement on Dale and she only wished she could have met him. Her mousey blonde hair and blue eyes were her only indication of what he looked like, as Leanne was a brunette with brown eyes, just like Chrissie.

The thought of Chrissie walking to school by herself sickened Hannah, to the point where she wanted to run after her mother and tell her what she thought of her. But what would it achieve? Besides, she would just get off her face and forget about everything anyway. That always seemed to be her solution.

Back before Dale, she had owned and run her parent's bakery and was an exceptional chef, often bringing home cookies and muffins for Hannah. Dale had come along and they had sold the bakery, meaning those days were long gone and Hannah found it hard to believe that she was still that same person. She had

had such passion and took such pride and joy in her work, now she was going downhill fast right before Hannah's eyes and there was nothing she could do to stop it.

Hannah could see though why her mum had fallen for Dale. 5 years ago he was tall, dark and handsome and his bad-boy demeanor could be seen as charming. He had swept Leanne right off her feet and she had failed to see him for what he really was. Now, all Hannah saw was a rotten, dark devil and she did everything in her power to steer clear of him. She had seen his 'bad' side all too often yet any time she had tried to get through to her mum, she had pushed her away, stood up for him and called Hannah a 'drama-queen'. It had hurt Hannah yet she couldn't let it get to her. She had to be stronger, for her sake and for Chrissie. It wouldn't be long before he turned on Chrissie too, because Dale was incapable of love. But he was damn good at acting, and Leanne believed his front and fell for his charm. Now, Leanne was beginning to see the signs, but she was in too deep to change and Hannah could sense things were about to get worse.

Hannah often had long thoughts about her situation, thoughts that a 15 year old shouldn't have to have. But she was only 15, what could she do?

At 3.10pm Hannah got ready to pick up her sister. She opted for her largest pair of sunnies that would best hide her face. She put them on and again grabbed her mirror. They weren't quite big enough, you could still see the bruising around the edge. She put on her hoodie, knowing how stupid she would look in 28 degree heat. But she didn't have much choice. She didn't want any questions.

Hannah would have to wait right outside Chrissie's classroom as Chrissie wouldn't be expecting her. It was a long walk and she hoped that Chrissie had made it ok. Thankfully it was only one long-winded road so she shouldn't have gotten lost, Hannah was more concerned though about the fact her 5 year old sister had been walking all by herself. The thought made her angry but she definitely wouldn't be feeling guilty. Her mum's job was to act like a mum. Hannah was acting like a big sister by picking her up.

Hannah could feel the sweat build up underneath her jumper as she waited outside Chrissie's classroom. She hoped the looks she was getting were because she was wearing a hoodie in the heat and not because people could see her shiner. *'Stupid Melbourne weather,'* she thought. It was ridiculous that it was this hot in the middle of April.

Chrissie raced straight out of the classroom and Hannah had to run after her. "Chrissie!" Hannah yelled, successfully getting her attention, but not before her teacher followed her out. "Chris, you forgot your schoolbag you silly duffer!" She went to hand it to her but Hannah instinctively took it from her. "Thanks," she said. Her teacher looked at Hannah disapprovingly. "It's a bit hot for a jumper on a day like today isn't it?"

"Mind your own...business," said Hannah, opting not to swear at Chrissie's teacher. "And its Chrissie, not Chris," she said as she placed Chrissie's bag on her own back. "Are you right then, little miss? Right to go home with... your sister I'm guessing?" She seemed to ignore Hannah's aggressive tone and continued on pleasantly to Chrissie. It made Hannah shudder. "Yup, this is my sister Hannah. Why *are* you wearing a jumper, Han, it's hot!" Hannah forced a smile. "No sense no feeling," she said and guided Chrissie away before her teacher could add a smart remark.

Chrissie skipped most of the way home, oblivious to Hannah's bruised face. Hannah had somehow pulled it off, she just wasn't sure she could hide it from Chrissie for the entire weekend. A bit of makeup would hopefully do the trick. They stepped inside the house and Hannah headed straight for the bathroom, ready to work on her transformation.

Once she'd finished with the foundation, Hannah checked her appearance one final time before exiting. The bruising was somewhat invisible but her eye itself was still bloodshot. There wasn't much she could do about that. She could hear Chrissie in the kitchen whining to her mum about the lack of food in the cupboard. As Hannah approached she saw Chrissie slip away with a snide smile, stuffing a packet of cookies into her pocket. Hannah pretended not to notice as she headed for her bedroom, when an exclamation from her sister made her heart sink. It was the simple scream of "Daddy's home!" that rattled Hannah to the point where she was sick to the stomach, and not because of the hunger that eating only mac and cheese all day can bring.

Dale opened the front door and was greeted by Chrissie who jumped into his arms. "Daddy!" she yelled. It was amazing to think Dale was her hero, someone she actually looked up to. Chrissie had no idea what Dale got up to, who he hung out with or what he did. And Hannah planned on keeping it that way, because if Chrissie knew, Hannah was afraid of what it might do to her. She had to protect her sister, even if it meant she wasn't looking after herself. Deep down Hannah knew it wasn't really doing her sister any favours either. But she didn't have much choice. If Dale was still her sister's idol, it meant he wasn't hurting her, and that, for now, was good enough for Hannah.

"I've got to show you something Daddy, wait here!" said Chrissie as she raced off to her bedroom. In Chrissie's temporary absence, Dale spotted Hannah and stepped over to her. Hannah felt her heart race and fear crept inside her, forcing her to freeze. He invaded her space by puffing his chest into her, making her feel small and useless. He looked down at her face and smirked. "No makeup to hide a red eye, is there Hannah?" he said with arrogance that enraged Hannah. She forced herself to look up into his eyes. She didn't say anything, she simply starred at him with all the hate she could muster. "I asked you a question," he said aggressively. Hannah sensed the danger of not responding to his rhetorical question, but she refused to give him the satisfaction. "We're out of milk," Leanne said. She had appeared around the corner. "Hi honey, I didn't know you were home. Hannah, go and get us some more milk would you?" So her mum had come to the rescue. Was it simply a coincidence or had she sensed the danger too? Hannah didn't care, all she knew was she needed to get out of the house, and if it meant walking 3km and back to get her mum milk, she would do it.

Hannah's stomach rumbled as she made her way to the milk bar and she spent the journey envisioning ways to get rid of Dale to distract herself from her immense hunger. Thoughts of poisoning him, of simply putting a gun to his head and pulling the trigger gave Hannah sheer satisfaction. But she was overcome with disappointment at the thought of explaining to her sister that she had killed her dad. Her thoughts were of course farfetched. For one she didn't have a gun and there were too many risks involved with poison. And she wasn't a killer. It was all pure fantasy, but it did the trick, it gave her a sense of happiness, even if it wasn't real.

Leanne had given Hannah $5, which was enough for milk and a little something else. Not that Leanne had intended for Hannah to spend the change on herself, but Hannah was starving, so she bought herself a chocolate bar to momentarily relieve her stomach.

Finally on the home stretch, Hannah approached her house, but she hesitated. Was she safe to return yet? She hadn't smelt any alcohol on Dale, which meant her chances of safety were increased, but he was clearly still in a foul mood with her. She wasn't exactly sure how he would react to returning with milk and no change either and she suddenly regretted spending the extra money. A little prolonged hunger was probably better than another black eye. Chrissie was home though which meant she was somewhat safe, although another half hour and she would be in bed. This was enough for Hannah to decide against delaying her return any longer, and she continued to the house.

She stepped inside and handed her mum the milk. Her mum lingered, clearly waiting for the change, but when Hannah didn't give it to her she said nothing and put the milk in the fridge. "Where's the rest of the money?" said Dale. Hannah had secretly hoped he would be dumb enough not to notice, but he was on a mission tonight. "They didn't give me any," Hannah replied, knowing all too well that it was a lame response. "Can't you fucking count you dumb bitch? How fucking stupid are you?" Hannah had to laugh to herself. So he was dumb enough to believe her. She had to laugh at the irony of him calling her stupid. She mustn't have been able to hide the smirk on her face as he again stepped in front of her. "You better start answering me when I ask you questions you little piece of scum or there'll be no dinner for you." She could handle the name calling, which really didn't bother her. She was used to it by now. But she so much wanted to tell him that she didn't care, because she had spent the money on a chocolate bar which would be far better than the dinner he served, but she bit her tongue.

She could see the anger in his eyes, she knew he wanted to hit her. But he had so far resisted with the presence of Chrissie in the house and awake, and Hannah prayed that it would still be enough. "Fine then. No dinner for you. *Bed,*" He demanded. Hannah wouldn't let him see the fear she felt. She looked into his face and forced herself to take a deep breath. "Fine by me," she said firmly. She walked away as quickly as she could, before he could stop her. She heard Chrissie enter the kitchen and ask where she was, but she shut the door before she could hear a reply. She was immediately hungry and she knew that whatever they were serving had to be better than a Mars bar.

Tiny footsteps and a knock on her door told Hannah her sister was outside her bedroom. She opened the door to find Chrissie in her pyjamas, holding her packet of cookies. "Here," said Chrissie, handing her the cookies. "No Chrissie, these are yours," Hannah pushed the biscuits away, but Chrissie refused. "No, take them Han, you haven't had any dinner." If she hadn't been so starving, she would have refused. Instead she gave her sister a big hug.

"Thanks kiddo. But it's not your fault I didn't have dinner you know,"

"I know, but it's what sisters are for." Hannah hugged her sister tight. *'Bless her,'* she thought. "Well, goodnight," said Chrissie and she left Hannah with her cookies. Hannah scoffed the cookies in a matter of seconds. She went to throw the wrapper in the bin, but instead she placed it inside her pillow case. Her one piece of kindness; she would hold on to it.

Amanda

Amanda arose from bed fresh and ready to take on the day ahead. It was Friday, thank goodness. Not that she hadn't enjoyed the week, teaching her preps the alphabet and listening to their interesting show-and-tell.

Heanwood Primary was definitely different to her last school, a completely different kettle of fish. There were no scholarships, no stand out students and certainly no unrealistic expectations and demands from parents. Her first semester had been one big eye opener in many respects. The kids in her class, more or less all of them, came from poor backgrounds where fancy cars and designer clothing were something from fantasy land.
Amanda had chosen to move to Heanwood simply because it meant she was closer to home. It had astounded her to think that a school like this was just around the corner from her lush and expensive suburb. One long road seemed to separate the rich from the poor. Her kids appreciated the move, though. It meant she got to spend longer with her daughter Jenna and she could pick Tyler up and take him to football training. It was easiest for her eldest son Cameron too, who had moved out the

year before and could pop 'round and babysit Jenna when required.

Amanda smiled as she thought of her children. Cam was following in his father's footsteps and completing his Masters in law. She was incredibly proud of him and the fact that at just 23, he was capable of moving out of home and settling in with his partner.

Then there was Tyler, who no doubt had his moments. But at 16 she came to expect the attitude that adolescence could bring. He could be hard at times, but he was a good kid.

That left little Jenna, her adorable 6 year old daughter. She could be a handful too, and Amanda probably let her get away with things a little too often. But she couldn't help it. Those curly locks, bright blue eyes and perhaps the fact she was a 'surprise' but an absolute blessing were factors that contributed to her being so spoiled.

Amanda glanced at the clock, registering that Danny would already have left for the city and Tyler and Jenna should both be out of bed. She gathered her gown and stepped into the lounge room to find Jenna glued to the TV. "Morning sunshine, is your brother up yet?" "Morning Mummy. He's still in bed."

Amanda sighed. Every day this week. She knocked on Tyler's door. "Tyler, honey, get up and get ready please."

"I'm not going."

"Are we really going to go through this again Ty?" No answer.

"Right, well if you're not going I guess we won't get pizza tonight then."

"I don't care."

"Really? Suit yourself then"

She pretended to call out to Jenna. "Jen, did you wanna try that new place down the road tonight, I hear they have the best ice cream? Yes? It'll just be the two of us." She could hear a thud behind the door. Food always did the trick.

Tyler opened the door. "What new place?" "Never mind honey. Great to see you up and ready, what can I get you for breakfast?" She gave him a wink and she could see the lightbulb click inside his head as he realised he'd been fooled out of bed yet again. But he continued to the kitchen and sat down at the table. Hard work, but a good kid.

Tyler had requested pancakes, so pancakes it was. She carefully poured Jenna's and worked her craft, forming it into the shape of a dinosaur. She scrambled her eggs and poured a generous amount of maple syrup. She playfully did the same to Tyler's, except his eggs were poached. She handed him his plate with a cheeky grin. "I'm not 5 mum" he said. "Don't eat it then" she replied. Jenna giggled and they both dug into their breakfast.

She dropped her kids off at school, kissed them goodbye and continued on her journey into work.

The day went by in a breeze, and she felt like she was finally earning respect from her students. As always it was the parents who proved most difficult and she was still getting her head around their different priorities. Their mums and dads just didn't seem to have the same level of care and it deeply concerned Amanda. At first she had put it down to the money situation, but that wasn't quite it. Because some of her students were worse off in terms of wealth, yet their parents did their very best and to Amanda, that was good enough. But some parents were simply never there. And some, well, if that was their best then that was worrying. It was the kids who lacked care factor that she had most trouble disciplining. They didn't take her seriously and they had clearly never taken orders from their parents. Amanda struggled with this handful, and when she approached these parents they told her where to go.

Her only drama for the day was when Lachie had another little incident involving his bladder. The first time this had happened it had been a catastrophe. The troubling kids had pointed and laughed, causing Lachie to cry which only made things worse. They had called him names and sent his confidence on a downward spiral, the poor kid was embarrassed beyond repair.

Not this time though, because Amanda was prepared now. She

always packed a couple of extra pairs of undies and as soon as she sensed Lachie go quiet, she took him to the bathroom and gave him her spare pair of jocks and a plastic bag. "Our little secret," she said and he whispered thank you as he headed for the cubicle.

The easiest solution for Lachie would be to start getting some control, and she knew having a spare pair of jocks handy might make it too easy for Lachie to bother trying. But it was these acts that had won over majority of her students, and besides, wetting your pants was something kids generally grew out of.

The bell to signal the end of the day was as exciting to Amanda as it was to her students. It meant her family would all be together that evening and she could hardly wait. She packed up Cindy's crayons as one by one, her students bade her goodbye and wished her a happy weekend. As she bent down to pick up the final crayon on the floor, she noticed Christina's bag still on its hook and she raced after her with it. Little Chris was so forgetful and she handed her her bag in a puff, before it was taken by a teenager wearing a hoodie, oblivious to the warm weather. She was sharp with Amanda when she questioned her attire and Amanda decided to leave it at that. As she looked into her face, hidden behind an extra large pair of sun glasses, Amanda sensed something off. Christina walked away with her sister and Amanda's mind began to race.
Teenagers didn't wear hoodies in hot weather. If anything, hot weather meant it was an excuse to wear less. Or was Amanda reading too much into it? Was it her sharp and aggressive tone towards Amanda that was causing her to jump to conclusions? She could have sworn she had seen a dark ring around the girl's eye, but she couldn't be certain because her sunglasses had shielded her face. She couldn't ignore it either and she thought about it all the way home. Christina was a shy and quiet girl, sometimes she was so quiet that Amanda almost forgot she was there. That worried Amanda now the more she thought about

it. And if her sister was hiding something, that affected Christina too. As her teacher, Amanda had a duty of care. She would keep a closer eye on Christina from now on.

CHAPTER 2

Hannah

Hannah stood and pushed Chrissie on the swing absent mindedly, subconsciously hearing Chrissie plead to go higher and higher. Hannah had taken Chrissie to the park more or less to get them both out of the house. The less time they spent in that place, the safer they would be. Weekends always possessed a greater danger, because Dale wasn't at work on weekends and he was a lot less predictable. Leanne was a lot worse on weekends too. She could spend every waking moment with Dale and that simply wasn't a good thing. He was dragging her under and Hannah couldn't help but wonder where she and her sister would go.

Hannah realised now, after the events of last night that she needed her own money. Money was freedom, a luxury Hannah couldn't yet afford. She suddenly stopped pushing Chrissie as an idea came to mind. She could vaguely recall seeing a vacancy sign at the café down the road. It was open until 5pm during the week and practically all day on weekends. Working on the weekend would be perfect. A waitress had certainly never been an appealing job to Hannah, but she didn't have many options. "Come on, Chrissie. Let's go for a walk." Chrissie obliged and jumped off the swing. She was such an easy kid.

Hannah came to a halt outside the café window, and, sure enough there was a "Waitress wanted" poster plastered on the glass. Hannah took a deep breath and checked her reflection through the window. She tucked her hair behind her ears and stepped inside, with Chrissie right behind. She had never enquired about a job before, but how hard could it be? She approached the counter. "Hi there, what can I get you today?" "Actually, er, I just wanted to ask about the waitress job advertised out the front?" The girl behind the counter looked a little surprised, and Hannah could feel her look her up and down. "Right, ok. Do you have your resume and I can pass it on to the manager?"

Hannah was puzzled. What on earth was a resume? She could tell by the girl's tone that she was expected to know what this was, not only to know but to have one as well. Maybe she should just leave before she embarrassed herself further. She decided to tell the truth. "Um, no sorry, I don't have one. Sorry to waste your time, I've never worked anywhere before."

The girl gave her a sympathetic smile. "That's ok. That explains why you don't have a resume. You could still write down your interests and any work experience you've done.. actually, our Manager Sarah has just come back now. What was your name?"

"Um, Hannah."

"Ok, just one sec." She smiled and headed out the back, returning with an older lady Hannah guessed to be Sarah. Hannah was suddenly very nervous and was regretting her decision, but Sarah smiled at her gently and it calmed her nerves.

"Hi Hannah, I hear you're interested in applying for the waitress position. Have you worked as a waitress before?"

"No, I've never actually worked anywhere before. I just thought I'd come in and ask. Sorry I don't have a resume." Sarah looked her up and down like the other girl, but she didn't feel like she was being judged. "I tell you what, don't worry about your resume. Can you come in tomorrow at 10am and we'll have a chat?" Hannah was taken aback. She had been expecting to be shown the door. "Um, sure that would be great, thanks."

"Perfect, I'll have Emma here exchange contact details and we'll see you at 10 o'clock tomorrow."

Sarah left Hannah with Emma and they exchanged phone numbers. "We've had this job advertised for weeks now. If you show up on time tomorrow you're in with a good shot"

Hannah thanked Emma and turned to leave. "Wait!" said Chrissie suddenly. Hannah had almost forgotten she was there. "Can I please get a muffin?" Chrissie asked. Hannah turned red, embarrassed again. "I don't have any money sorry, Chrissie," she whispered. "I do!" said Chrissie and she pulled out her little purse. So her 5 year old sister got pocket money, yet she didn't get anything. Hannah had never wanted to be a waitress so badly.

"So what was all that about?" asked Chrissie as she walked along happily munching on her blueberry muffin. "I applied to be a waitress. I go back for an interview tomorrow," replied Hannah. "You'd be great at it Han!" said Chrissie enthusiastically. Hannah appreciated her positivity. Though from a biased 5 year old, she would take it. She certainly wasn't going to get it from anyone else. The thought made Hannah sigh. She couldn't help the way things were with her mum and Dale, but they had a lot to do with how she acted at school. She didn't exactly mean to take it out on her teachers, but they didn't understand her and they expected so much from her. How could she explain to them that her mum's stupid boyfriend had lit up her homework with his cigarette lighter to amuse his friends? It sounded lamer than the dog eating it. Plus it was something an older brother would do, not an adult and certainly not someone presumed to care about her. It was best for everyone if they just thought she was a dumb, troubled teen set for rebellion. They didn't like it, but they would accept it. She could handle being pestered for homework, she couldn't deal with questions about her family life. She had nowhere else to go.

Hannah and Chrissie headed back to the park for the afternoon, but Hannah was hungry and she couldn't prolong going back to the house any longer. As they entered their street, Hannah recognised three cars parked outside their house. They belonged to Dale's friends who all enjoyed giving Hannah a hard time. Oblivious to Hannah's apprehension to go back, Chrissie raced ahead. "Last one to the house is a rotten egg!" She yelled. Hannah jogged after her, she really shouldn't be letting her enter the house first.

She followed Chrissie to the house and stepped inside. She could hear loud voices in the backyard. Hannah knew only too well what they were up to.

Her mum was in the kitchen washing the dishes. Chrissie had raced straight to her bedroom.

"I can't believe you let those guys do that here," said Hannah before she could stop herself. "Oh Han, stop being a sook. It's harmless."

"You have a 5 year old daughter!"

"Oh, so you care about your sister today do you? Didn't care about her yesterday."

Her mum was clearly under the influence too.

"Get a grip, take a look in the mirror," Hannah yelled. She wasn't helping the situation, just stooping to her mother's low levels. "Loosen up Han, you should get out there and join in. have a joint. Haha get it? Join in and have a joint."

Hannah just starred at her mum, almost pitying her. What had she become? What had Dale turned her into?

Her mum continued on washing the dishes and Hannah noticed her pick up a plate she had just washed, and re-wash it. Hannah could take it no longer, she headed back to her bedroom when the back door opened. Dale entered followed by his friend Scott. "Hey Hannah! Come join us!" said Scott. "No, thanks," said Hannah. "Nah, Hannah's much too cool to hang out with us," said Dale as he stumbled over the back step. Hannah rolled her eyes almost automatically. "See what I mean?" Dale continued as Scott sniggered. "Daddy!" exclaimed Chrissie as she ran out of her bedroom. "Hey missy, where have you been?"

"Han took me to the park, and, she's going to be a waitress!" Hannah's heart sank. She hadn't exactly worked out how she would tell her mum and Dale if she got the job, but she certainly wasn't planning on telling them she was going for an interview.

Dale's friends sniggered loudly and Dale stepped in close, invading her space once again. "Who'd want to be served by a skank like you? You'll send the place broke. Then again, waitressing is probably a good thing, it's probably all you'll ever do."

Hannah's temper was rising and it got the better of her before she could control it. "Coming from a piece of shit for brains like you? What exactly have you done? Sell our family's bakery so you can buy drugs and sell them to 15 year olds? Bravo."

She could feel her heart pounding in her chest and she was so angry she was surprised she'd got the words out, but she knew she shouldn't have done it. She couldn't afford to make Dale and his friends angry. "You're not gunna put up with that tramp speaking to you like that are you mate?" asked Scotty provocatively. They were inching closer now and Hannah felt helplessly trapped. Her mum was too far gone to intervene and she felt ashamed to hope her 5 year old sister might step in and save the day.

Dale placed his right hand on Hannah's throat and she closed her eyes, not wanting to look at his evil face. "That wasn't very nice," he said as he tightened his grip slightly. He looked her up and down and used his free hand to slide it up her top. She opened her eyes, she hadn't been expecting that. He grinned and before she could do anything he shoved her viciously against the wall. The back of her head slammed against the plaster and she felt dazed, out of it. She felt as if her ears were partially blocked and she couldn't think straight. She could vaguely hear Chrissie's voice, but she sounded so far away. Hannah blinked, trying to regain focus. She couldn't hear or feel Dale near her and she couldn't pin point where he and his friends had gone. She needed to get to her bedroom as quickly as possible, before they returned. She stumbled out of the kitchen and into the hallway, managing to find her way to her door. As she turned the door handle she felt a hand on her back, but before she could comprehend what was happening she received another forceful shove, this time knocking her forehead into her bedroom door. Whether it was because her head had already received a heavy knock, or because this hit was much harder, her brain couldn't handle the force and she was knocked out of consciousness, vulnerable and with no way to defend herself.

Amanda

Amanda woke to the sound of running water, indicating that Tyler was up and on the move for his football match. She smiled to herself. He couldn't get out of bed for school, but he could be up at 7.00am on the weekend to play sport. She loved watching him play, but not as much as Danny did. This was their thing. No doubt Danny would be playing out set plays in his head, even though he had given up his coaching duties the year before. It had been too hard with his work and now that Tyler was in Under 16s, things were starting to get a lot more serious and Danny just couldn't commit to the hours required. Amanda rolled over and hugged her husband tight. He was already awake with his arms resting underneath his head. "Tyler's up," she said. "Don't make him pancakes this morning honey, not after all that ice cream last night. Bacon and eggs would be better."

Amanda had to laugh to herself, she thought cereal would have been the better option, but what did she know?

She rose up out of bed and pulled back the curtains. Danny got up immediately to assess the weather conditions. They were the complete opposite to yesterdays.

Amanda made her way to the kitchen and began preparing breakfast. Tyler sat down at the table, fresh from his morning shower. "How are you feeling today Ty?" He shrugged his shoulders and yawned. Yawning was a sign of nerves for Tyler and he always got them before he played. Danny entered the room and patted Tyler on the shoulder. "You'll be right bud, it's wet outside, perfect conditions for you today."

It was true, for some reason Tyler always played better in the rain. It was like everyone else's skills dropped a level, yet his increased. This seemed to relax Tyler and he grabbed the morning paper. Tyler never read anything, unless it was sport related and within 24 hours before he played. Amanda smiled to herself again. Footy was now good for two things. Thinking back to the first, she realised Jenna wasn't at the table. "Is your sister not up yet?" she asked. "Nope. I'm about to go jump on her actually."

"I'll take care of it, said Danny with a wink and he headed for Jenna's bedroom. They could hear Jenna's squeals, the sound of laughter and within 30 seconds Danny returned with Jenna on his shoulders. Jenna was still in hysterics and it took skill from Danny not to drop her as she leant back, laughing uncontrollably.

He sat her down on the table and kissed her on the head. "Little Jenna the terror was hiding under the covers, but you didn't hear daddy coming, did ya?" Jenna shook her head and giggled. "How many goals am I gunna kick today Jen?" asked Tyler. "Four!" Replied Jenna. The funny thing was, Jenna had been right in guessing the last two times Tyler had asked, meaning she was on a hat trick. 4 goals would be a tough ask on a day like today. Tricky weather and good opposition. "I'll see what I can do," said Tyler.

Danny parked the car along the fence so that Amanda and Jenna could watch from the car – he would no doubt stand next to the coach's box so he could add in his two cents. As Danny and Tyler headed for the club rooms, Jenna climbed into the front seat next to her mum and they got themselves comfortable for the game.

Tyler ran out with his teammates and Amanda beeped the horn. "Let's go Tigers!" she yelled and Jenna clapped. No one could hear them but it didn't matter, it was Amanda's favourite part of the week. The game played out as predicted, a tight contest with the Tigers marginally in front. Tyler was also dominating as predicted and had kicked 2 goals to half time, on target for 4.

The opposition came out hard in the third term and kicked the opening 2 goals to put them back in front. Tyler managed to break free from his direct opponent and he took a good mark 30 metres out from goal. It was a tough angle, but he used the wind to his advantage and the ball swung back nicely, sailing through the middle. He made his way back to the centre and copped a few heavy knocks as his opponents tried to rattle him. He had been on top all day and they needed to stop him. What they didn't realise was this tactic often had the opposite effect – it caused Tyler to play on adrenalin and his game went up a notch.

Amanda adjusted herself in her seat and focused on Tyler. "Ready Jenna, I think goal number 4 might be coming up," she said. A couple of players went for Tyler at the next bounce, but he was agile and one step ahead. He swung around quickly, side stepped and sprinted to the forward line, leaving both opponents for dead. The ball sailed high in the air and Tyler braced himself for the mark, clearly wanting the lead up to his 4th goal to be spectacular. He jumped up on his teammates' shoulders and grabbed the ball, but his teammate leant forward and Tyler was suspended in mid-air. It happened as if in slow motion. He somehow managed to hold on to the ball, despite the weather, but what comes up must come down, and he fell back down to earth with a heavy blow. His head hit first and the momentum from his body meant he hit the ground hard. His body landed awkwardly and he didn't move. Amanda gasped and charged out of the car, wanting to enter the ground to her son but knowing she couldn't. The trainers rushed over and Amanda held her breath, feeling both scared and helpless.

"Will he be ok?" asked Jenna who had followed her mum out from the car. "He'll…he'll be fine, he'll be fine," replied Amanda. She had to remain calm for Jenna's sake. Danny had followed the trainers onto the ground, he was practically still part of the club anyway.

He returned moments later and hugged Amanda. "He's breathing, they've called an ambulance, he'll be fine," he added as he saw the look on his daughter's face.

Amanda sat with Tyler in the ambulance while Danny and Jenna followed behind. He had moved but he hadn't regained consciousness. The paramedics had reassured Amanda that he would be fine, but she still felt sick. As they pulled up to the hospital, Tyler opened his eyes. "Mum?" he whispered. She got up and smiled with relief. "You're ok Ty, you're just at the hospital. You went for a mark and you landed on your head. How do you feel?" He was quiet for a moment, before answering with a typical response. "Did we win?" She laughed. "It doesn't matter, it just matters that you're ok." He thought about it. "I'd feel better if we won."

The paramedics took Tyler on a stretcher into the hospital and Amanda was again joined with Danny and Jenna. "He's ok, he's awake," she said. "How is he?" asked Danny. "He's fine. He wants to know if they won."

They entered the hospital and sat in the waiting area. They were greeted by the doctor who advised them that Tyler appeared to be ok, but that they would keep him overnight as a precaution. Tyler was greeted with hugs from his family as he lay watching TV. "I have to stay overnight," he said, annoyed. "It will be fine Ty, they're just making sure you're ok."

"I am ok. I just wish we'd won," he said. He was more disappointed with the loss than how he felt physically. "Well, Ben kicked the goal after you went off, so I think that still counts as 4 goals," said Jenna matter-of-factly. Tyler smiled. "And how was the mark Jen, good?" "It was a specie!" she said. Tyler smiled and rolled over, seemingly satisfied now.

CHAPTER 3

Hannah

Hannah awoke in a daze, unsure where she was or how she got there. She struggled to open her eyes and her pounding head was making it difficult to want to. Had she been dreaming? How long had she been asleep? What day was it? She forced her eyes open and recognised the digital clock by her bedside. It told her that it was 11.15 and judging by the light, it was definitely AM, not PM. Hannah tried to think about the past few hours, and how she had come to be in bed, but thinking made her head hurt. She was suddenly made aware of an ache in her chest and as she attempted to adjust her bra, she realised that it was undone. This confused her further. Why had she fallen asleep in her clothes in the first place? She stretched out her legs and realised that while she was still wearing her t-shirt and bra, she wasn't wearing any pants, just her underwear.

Hannah sat up and the sudden movement made her head spin. She gasped in pain and held her head in her hands. Why couldn't she remember? She forced herself out of bed to take a look in the mirror. She had strange marks across her throat and chest with no idea how they got there. "Hannah?" a little voice at the door snapped Hannah out of her thoughts. She pulled out a pair of trackies and a jumper, put them on and opened the door. She looked down at Chrissie, ready to pretend she was fine. "What's up?" she asked. "Why didn't you go to your interview?" 'Interview, interview…' Hannah racked her brains and as she said it a third time it all came rushing back. Dale and his friends had made fun of her when they had found out about her interview, Dale had hit her against the wall and she'd rushed to the bedroom. Hannah tried to think what had happened next. Did she enter? Did she simply fall asleep? How the hell did she sleep so long? She went back to her room and grabbed her phone. 4 missed calls. Shit! And a voicemail message. She dreaded listening to it. She had blown it.

"What were you doing with Daddy and his friends anyway?" Chrissie asked and Hannah felt immediately sick. What was she talking about?

"What do you mean?" she asked, dreading the answer. "You were all in here," Chrsissie said. Hannah was confused, but as she thought about the marks she had seen in the mirror she struggled to breathe. What had they done to her? Hannah felt sick and she raced to the bathroom. She vomited violently and as she did so she recalled banging her head against her bedroom wall, right before she had felt hands on her back.

She had been knocked unconscious, she probably had concussion. For all she knew she was lucky to be alive. *Lucky*, she smirked. Was she really? She'd almost rather the alternative than being stuck in this house. Especially now, after what had potentially happened. *'It couldn't have,'* she thought. Surely she would know. But she had been unconscious.

She returned to her bedroom where Chrissie was still standing. She looked unusual, like a deer in the headlights. "Chrissie, are you ok?" She nodded, but continued to look dazed. "Are you sure kiddo, you look like you've seen a ghost." Chrissie didn't say anything. She looked at Hannah. "You looked like a ghost last night," she said. Hannah wanted to ask Chrissie what she had seen, to know what happened. But then, what *had* Chrissie seen, and should she really be making her re-live it?

Hannah suddenly felt disgusting, like she had been thrown in the mud and hadn't showered. She wanted to remove herself from her body. To shed her skin and move into a new, clean one. One that hadn't been violated. And then she knew. And her body ached all over. She couldn't look at Chrissie, couldn't bear to think what she had seen.

"I don't feel very well Chrissie, please just leave me alone for a while."

"Can I get you some water? Panadol?"

"No, just, please leave."

"I can help."

"No, you can't. Just get out." She raised her voice and she hated herself for doing it. But she was angry, upset and helpless. She didn't know what to do. She stepped back into her room and stood once again in front of her mirror. She hated everything she saw. Her body, her useless situation, her eyes that belonged to someone she had never known, someone she desperately wanted to meet but who clearly wanted nothing to do with her. Why couldn't she just be somebody else, anybody else? Anybody had to be better than the small, insignificant person she saw starring back at her. She grabbed her phone and listened to her voicemail message. She had expected Sarah to be angry and abusive, yet she sounded concerned and worried. It was the care in Sarah's voice that got to Hannah.

She crouched down on her floor and hugged herself. She hugged herself so tight she couldn't breathe. Why did someone she had met briefly for 5 minutes show compassion when she experienced such hate from those who were meant to show love? She rocked back and forth as the stream of tears began to fall.

Amanda

Tyler was re-assessed and released from hospital by Sunday afternoon and he sat on the couch watching TV with his sister. Amanda was busy in the kitchen preparing dinner. Relieved that her son was ok, she thought she would celebrate by cooking his favourite meal; roast lamb with mash and veggies. She smiled to herself knowing she would have no trouble getting Tyler out of bed for school tomorrow. He would thoroughly enjoy the attention he would receive from his classmates who had witnessed his game. Although she could probably keep him home, tomorrow she would struggle to stop him from running out the door. Jenna had no trouble either, she adored school and the new friends she had made. Suddenly, the thought of Jenna caused Amanda to think of her own students who were of similar age, and she remembered her promise to herself to keep an eye on Chrissie. She would pay close attention to her tomorrow.

Hannah

Hannah remained in her bed all day, too scared to leave. She had cried herself to sleep which had been a mistake. Her tears had caused an even bigger headache and she was beginning to feel increasingly sick. It was after 8pm and she realised she hadn't eaten a thing all day. She could smell burnt toast which indicated dinner had been toasted sandwiches, the melted cheese was one of her favourite things. She decided she would sneak out to the bathroom and at least drink some water from the tap. As she made her way silently towards the bathroom, she could hear Dale speaking to her mum.

"I'm gunna be at home this week babe. Scott's coming 'round and we need to sort out some stuff. Be good if you were around to make lunch for us." Hannah could hear her mum sigh. "What am I, your slave? You make your own lunch."

She said it half sarcastically, but Dale's tone changed. "You're the woman of the house, you make the lunch, I provide. It's that simple, you got it?" It was another rhetorical question and one that Leanne answered quickly. "Ok, ok, got it."

You weak piece of nothing,' thought Hannah, although she couldn't really blame her. The alternative option wasn't pretty. Hannah sighed to herself. Dale being home meant she had no choice but to go to school. She simply couldn't be in the house with him and if she skipped school again Chrissie would ask questions. Besides, where would she go anyway? It appeared that Chrissie had respected Hannah's wishes and had stayed away. Hannah regretted this now as another packet of cookies would have gone down well. She would make an effort to be as normal as possible towards Chrissie tomorrow in the hope that her memories of the weekend would be forgotten.

CHAPTER 4

Hannah

As Hannah walked with Chrissie to school she felt completely out of it, but despite her throbbing headache she tried to act normal. It was Chrissie who wasn't her usual self, she was extremely quiet. "You ok kiddo?" asked Hannah. "Yup" replied Chrissie, short and sharp. As they reached the classroom gate Hannah saw Chrissie's teacher waiting at the door. Hannah decided not to walk any further, she didn't appreciate the disapproving look she received last time. "Ok well, you have a good day ok and just, be good ok?" Like she had to tell her to be good. She didn't really even know why she said it, but she felt awkward and had horrible visions of them all sitting in a circle telling their 'show and tell' stories. Hannah cringed at the thought of what Chrissie might say.

Chrissie's teacher waved at Hannah as she greeted Chrissie, but Hannah chose to ignore her and headed to the senior part of the school. Hannah was still in a daze and her headache meant she walked slower as she tried to concentrate on where she was going. As she entered the classroom she found an empty desk at the back of the room and attempted to refocus her eyes which were struggling to see. She really shouldn't be here. Any normal person would have asked her mum to take her to the doctors. Any normal person wouldn't have a headache for the reasons she did and wouldn't need to be taken to the doctors in the first place. Hannah was a million miles away as she contemplated a different life, a place where she was free from the fear of her own home.

"Hannah, that's 3 times I've said your name now, would it be so hard as to respond!?" Hannah snapped out of her daydream and starred at her teacher, oblivious that she had been taking roll call. Her teacher starred back at her with an impatient look upon her face. "You were absent Friday Hannah, or were you actually here and didn't bother to say anything?"

Hannah was having trouble reading her teacher's tone and body language. Was she supposed to answer that or was she being sarcastic? *'No, I was at home Friday thanks to a black eye, and I shouldn't even be here today given what happened,'* she thought to herself. Her teacher was beginning to get frustrated now. "Stop being ridiculous Hannah, are you a mute? A simple 'yes' response isn't that hard, even for you, surely?"

Hannah could feel herself getting angry now. She could barely stand being belittled at home, she didn't need to be made to feel small here too. "Well it's pretty bloody obvious I'm here, isn't it? You're speaking to me, just mark me down as here. It's not that hard, even for you, surely?"

She mimicked her teacher and while she knew she shouldn't have said what she said, she couldn't help the sense of satisfaction she felt at the fact she could say what she wanted with no consequence. Because as much as she might want to, her teacher couldn't lay a hand on her. It felt so good to let out her frustration and she immediately felt the tension ease a little. Besides, she thought she had a point anyway. Her teacher could see she was here, why did Hannah have to say so? *'Dumb idiot,'* she thought to herself.

Her teacher chose to ignore Hannah and continued with calling the rest of the class, but she pulled Hannah aside before she headed to her first subject. "I really don't appreciate your attitude Hannah. Everyone else can follow the rules, why can't you? Why is it so difficult for you to reply, it's easy enough for everyone else?" Hannah sighed to herself. '*Maybe because no one else gets assaulted by their step dad, ever thought about that?*'

Oh what she would give to see the look on her teacher's face if she actually said it, but she couldn't. What would her teacher care? She'd probably think it served her right for being such a smart alec. Hannah just stared back at her teacher. She was in a lose-lose no matter what she said, so why bother? "I don't have time for this Hannah, just get to class," said her teacher with a hint of frustration in her voice. '*Suits me,*' thought Hannah as she walked away. She had gotten off lightly and Hannah felt a little better in herself. She wondered how far she could push the limits in her next class.

Hannah made her way to her first class of the day. Her headache kept coming and going and it made it hard for her to concentrate. Her entire body was sore and she made her way in slow motion. Everyone was in slow motion mode anyway, it was Monday and they were all catching up with their friends and exchanging stories about the weekend. This was something Hannah no longer experienced. She had had many friends once, and back in primary school she had actually been popular. But she had grown apart, her friends had all grown up, they liked going to each other's houses and attending parties on the weekends. This wasn't an option for Hannah. She couldn't possibly have friends over, her mum and Dale wouldn't let her and she didn't want anyone to come over anyway. Plus, she was never allowed to go to parties and there was no one to take her to them. Hannah had become a bit of an outsider, she didn't go to parties so she wasn't cool and she would never stoop to her mum's levels and take drugs so she wasn't part of that crowd either. She was a recluse, she didn't fit in. She had one friend, her best friend Tess, and they generally sat together. Tess didn't exactly fit in either, what with her jet black hair and tattoos. She was different and Hannah could sense she'd had a difficult time at home too, but they didn't judge one another and that simply made them friends.

"Hey," said Tess as Hannah spotted her and sat down. "'Sup," replied Hannah as she rested her head in her right hand. "How was your weekend?" asked Tess. "Shithouse, you?" "Ditto," she replied. They smiled at each other and that was the end of the conversation.

Despite the joy Hannah would have got out of tormenting her English teacher, Hannah didn't say a word all class as she struggled to keep her eyes open. As the bell sounded Tess gave her a nudge. "Hannah? You just slept through that entire class! What exactly did you do on the weekend!?"

"You don't want to know," said Hannah flatly as thoughts of yesterday entered her mind. "Are you ok?" asked Tess, concerned. Hannah said nothing. *'Define 'ok'*" she thought. Had she ever really been ok? She couldn't remember the last time she'd felt even remotely ok.

As Hannah looked at her diary she realised she had a free period. "Sweet, no class!" she exclaimed. The idea of taking a nap under a tree was suddenly very appealing. "No way!" said Tess as she grabbed Hannah's diary. "Screw that I've got maths, I'm having a free class too," said Tess as she handed Hannah back her diary. "Fine by me, but I was gunna go have a nap," said Hannah. "Screw that!" Tess said again. "You have a better idea?" asked Hannah. "Actually.." Tess had that look on her face now. "Follow me," she said with a grin.

Hannah followed Tess to her locker hoping that whatever her idea was was exceptionally good. Tess pulled out a pack of cigarettes and a water bottle. Hannah starred at the cigarettes, unimpressed. "Well, you know you're struggling when you get this excited over a packet of Winston's," said Hannah tonelessly. "Not just cigarettes, Han," said Tess as she waved her drink bottle next to her head. Hannah suddenly put two and two together. "Alcohol Tess? Really? It's like, not even 10 o'clock in the morning."

Tess sighed. "Fine, you go have your nap. But if you change your mind, I'll be behind the old portables." Hannah said nothing. "Ok Han, so maybe the alcohol's a little heavy, but you really look like you need it, even if it's just to forget about yesterday, or the weekend, or whatever."

Again, Hannah just starred at her blankly, indecisive. "I can't even tempt you with one of these?" Tess said as she held out a fag. Hannah said nothing. Tess sighed again, appearing to give up. She exited the locker bay and headed in the direction of the portables. While Hannah longed for a sleep, she couldn't get the image of a quick puff out of her head and she followed Tess to the portables.

Hannah and Tess sat with their backs against the portable, Tess taking swigs from her bottle and Hannah smoking her cigarette. Hannah always found it a little ironic that one quick puff made it instantly easier for her to breathe. She hated that they eased her stress, but she loved it at the same time. Hannah sighed to herself. "God we're lame," she said as she turned to Tess, watching her drink straight vodka from the bottle. Tess smiled at her. "Speak for yourself," she said with a wink as she took one extra-large mouthful. Hannah gave her a playful shove and she missed her mouth, spilling a few drops onto herself. "Now I'm gunna smell like vodka!" Tess yelled and she started laughing uncontrollably. "Give me that," said Hannah, taking the bottle from Tess. "If you can't beat 'em, join 'em," said Tess with a grin, hinting at Hannah to have a swig. Hannah considered that statement. She peered into the bottle and stared at the liquid below. Tess's laughter filled Hannah's ears. She shrugged her shoulders and poured the remaining vodka into her mouth.

Hannah and Tess didn't move from their position behind the portables for the next hour. Hannah sat in silence, debating whether to fill Tess in on the weekend's 'activities'. But every time she opened her mouth to speak, she couldn't think what to say. Where could she start, what would Tess think? How did she even feel? It was all too confusing and way too complicated. Besides, Tess was busily texting someone back and forth and Hannah didn't feel like disturbing her. She was certain Tess wouldn't be interested or care about what she had to say anyway. It really was a pathetic situation. Hannah needed to tell someone though, and Tess was the only person on the planet she could possibly tell. Maybe she would just have to bite the bullet and tell her. She started counting to 5 in her head, when she got to 5, she would start talking and just go with it. "1, 2, 3...4...4 and a half.." "I'm going to meet up with Jack at tea break - want to join?" asked Tess as her thumbs worked at lightning speed. Hannah didn't particularly feel like meeting up with Jack and his friends. She wasn't in the mood, plus she definitely didn't want to say anything in front of boys. What she had to say was for Tess's ears only, not that she even knew where to begin. "Not really," said Hannah. "Suit yourself. Well, if things are too weird at home, you should come to mine after school. I'll be at the park opposite the playground for a bit, then I'll head home. If you're not there by 5 I won't wait around, but the offer's there. My parents won't be home."

Tess got up out of her position, tucked her phone in her pocket and put out her cigarette. "See ya later."

Tess left Hannah alone with her thoughts. She sighed. She hated feeling so alone, yet she didn't want to be surrounded by people either. She should have told Tess.

She stretched her legs and held the empty drink bottle in her hands. Why did things have to be like this? Why did Dale have to come into their lives? He had ruined everything and now things had become so much worse. She thought about going home. She hated everything about that stupid house. The faded white picket fence, the foul smell, the creaky floorboards and the people in it. She hated them all, everyone except Chrissie. Poor little Christina. Hannah wondered again exactly what she had seen. She definitely couldn't talk to her about it, but she must be confused. It was too much for a 5 year old's mind. Hannah grasped her hands tightly around the bottle and before she knew what she was doing, she threw it as far as she could. The bottle landed with a thud and filled Hannah with a momentary sense of relief. She looked at her watch. Tea break was just about over. She got up and made her way over to the bottle. She would return it to Tess when she met her at the park. She would head there straight after she'd dropped off Chrissie at that god awful place she called home.

Amanda

Amanda was having a good morning. Tyler had bounced out of bed as predicted, Jenna had been her usual happy self and Danny had promised to be home in time for dinner. She had arrived at work at 8.30 on the dot which gave her ample time to get the classroom in order for the day. Her class had started in typical Monday-morning fashion as her students sat in a circle with their souvenirs from the weekend. Cindy had stolen the show when it was her turn and her mum had popped in with a brand new bunny. The class had gone into melt down and Amanda couldn't help feeling pleased that a furry animal was the cause of much love and joy no matter what background you were from. Perhaps the only student who hadn't attempted to pat Bugsy was Chrissie who remained in her spot in the circle while everyone else had jumped up to pat the rabbit. Amanda had been meaning to ask Chrissie if she had an allergy but she was interrupted by Cindy's mum who wanted to point out how far advanced her little angel was.

Once the class had settled down it was time to move to activity number 2 and Amanda began walking around the room, handing each student a colouring book. They all took out their pencils and Amanda sat back down at her desk, glancing occa-

sionally at her class as they sat busily colouring in their pictures. As she moved her eyes between each student, she couldn't help but notice Chrissie who sat absent-mindedly, her colouring was going well and truly outside the lines. Amanda focused on Chrissie who appeared to be a million miles away. She got up off her chair and made her way over to Chrissie. The 5 year old didn't seem to notice her teacher hovering over her and she continued to colour her sun blue. "Chrissie, honey are you ok?" Asked Amanda as she knelt down beside her. Chrissie didn't move, she simply continued colouring. "Chrissie?" Amanda tried again. "Is something bothering you? You don't seem to be paying much attention to your colouring."
There was more silence before Chrissie mumbled "I have a stomach ache."
 She didn't look up, her head was face down and her nose was nearly touching the paper. "Would you like to go to sick bay?" Chrissie shook her head. "How about I call your mum, is she home today?" Chrissie gave no reply, leaving Amanda puzzled.
She made her way to her office and pondered giving Chrissie's mother a call. Clearly something wasn't ok and she didn't know what to do.
She took out her students' medical files and began searching for Chrissie's contact details. She found her home number, picked up the phone and began to dial. The phone rang several times and just as Amanda was about to hang up, she heard movement on the other end.
"Hello?" "Er, hi this is Mrs Carson, Christina's teacher. Is this Leanne?" "Yes, what do you want?" Amanda was still having trouble getting used to her new students and their families, yet she wasn't expecting that response, or the aggressive tone.
"Er, it's about Christina, you see she said she has a stomach ache and I was wondering.." "Well send her to sick bay, you're her teacher, what are you calling me for?" Before Amanda could respond, Leanne had hung up. Amanda pulled the phone away from her ear and starred at it in disbelief. The lack of care or remote sign of concern was alarming. Before she knew what she

was doing, she hit re-dial. This time, the phone was answered straight away. "Yes?" said a male voice. "Hi, this is Mrs Carson.." "Would you stop calling us about a stupid stomach ache? Tell Chrissie to deal with it and her sister will pick her up after school. Don't bother us again. BYE." Amanda was hung up on for the second time.

She placed the phone down and peered out of her office at Chrissie who had stopped colouring and was starring blankly out the window.
Something was not right. Amanda decided to try a new tactic.
"Chrissie, can you please come here for a minute?" she asked. Chrissie put her pencil down and made her way slowly to her teacher's office. "How's your tummy?" Amanda asked. "It's ok," said Chrissie as she looked down at her feet. "Are you sure?" Chrissie nodded. "Ok, well is there anything else bothering you? Anything at all? You know you can tell me if there is."
Amanda knelt down beside Chrissie but Chrissie wouldn't look up. She continued to stare at her feet. Amanda took the continued silence as an opportunity to inspect Chrissie, but there was no sign of anything unusual, no strange markings or bruising. Amanda hated herself for presuming the worst, but she had been warned about the higher risk of abuse since moving to her new school. "I phoned home. Your dad said your sister would pick you up after school." Amanda noticed a momentary change in body language but she couldn't quite put her finger on it. Did she sense fear inside Chrissie when she mentioned she had phoned home, or was she just being paranoid? "Can I go back to my seat now?" asked Chrissie. "Of course you can."
Amanda followed Chrissie back to the classroom and sat behind her desk.

Amanda spent the afternoon reliving her bizarre phone calls and pondering what they meant. She found it unusual too that both parents would be home at the same time during the day. What were they up to and what was more important than their daughter's well-being?

Amanda glanced again at Chrissie's file and noticed that both her parent's job descriptions were undisclosed. *'How convenient,'* thought Amanda. The more she thought about it, the more suspicious Amanda became. Plus there was Chrissie's older sister who also appeared to have something to hide. Amanda would assess Chrissie again tomorrow, and if something wasn't right, she would investigate further.

Her gut was telling her that something just didn't add up.

CHAPTER 5

Hannah

As the bell sounded at 3.00pm, Hannah packed up her things and made her way to Chrissie's classroom. Her headache wouldn't go away and she wondered now if the alcohol had been such a good idea. She waited by the gate outside the classroom as every one of Chrissie's classmates departed, everyone except Chrissie. Hannah was growing impatient, she wanted to meet with Tess as soon as possible.
Hannah suddenly spotted Chrissie who was accompanied by her teacher. "Come on, Chrissie!" shouted Hannah. Chrissie walked towards Hannah with her teacher beside her. "It's Hannah right?" asked Chrissie's teacher. Hannah rolled her eyes at her but didn't respond. Instead she grabbed Chrissie's school bag and ushered for her to hurry up. "Wait a minute. Your sister wasn't feeling well today, I tried phoning home but your parents, well, they said you would pick her up," "And that's what I'm doing. If you don't mind, I'm in a hurry."
 Hannah couldn't help her aggressive tone. She really couldn't understand why this teacher was attempting to make conversation with her anyway. Couldn't she see she had places to go?
"I'm just looking out for her wellbeing. Just keep an eye on her, ok?" "Thanks for the advice. Come on Chrissie, let's go." She turned her back on Chrissie's teacher and they left.

Once they were on their way, Hannah knelt down to speak to her sister. "What's the go with your teacher? What's her name anyway?" "Her name is Mrs Carson, I told her I had a tummy ache. She's nice." Hannah considered that for a moment. Chrissie said she *told* her teacher she had a tummy ache, she didn't say she *had* a stomach ache. "Is everything ok, kiddo?" she asked reluctantly. Chrissie nodded and kept walking. Clearly everything wasn't ok and she couldn't even talk to her teacher about it. That was probably a good thing, this Mrs Carson seemed nosey and Hannah didn't like it. She should mind her own business. Of course, she had every right to be concerned for her student, but Hannah didn't need anyone poking around their private life. It would just lead to more trouble.

As Hannah and Chrissie stepped inside their house, Hannah stuck to her plan and headed straight for her bedroom. She grabbed her pillow and a backpack and stuffed fresh school uniform and pyjamas into her bag. She wasn't sure if she would end up staying, but she wanted to give herself the option. She made her way to the bathroom to grab her toothbrush, but loud shouts from the kitchen made her freeze.
Dale was yelling at Chrissie, something Hannah had never heard him do before. Her protective instincts took over and she followed the sounds to the kitchen. Dale's voice was echoing throughout the room. "Haven't I taught you anything? Grow up Chrissie, you don't go running off to your teacher if you have a little stomach ache. Your mum and I are busy, we don't expect to be telephoned during the middle of the day, ok? Not for petty shit like that."
Chrissie was in tears. "I'm sorry, I didn't tell her to phone."
"What did you think she was going to do, you silly girl?" Hannah couldn't believe what she was hearing. Why all the commotion over something so small? She looked at Dale and it was plain to see he was under the influence, his eyes were blood shot and he was having trouble standing straight. Leanne was standing next to him and Hannah could tell she also wasn't in her normal state. She was nodding in agreement alongside Dale. What on earth was going on? "Just go to your room," Dale ordered. Chris-

sie just stood there, utterly bewildered. "I *said* GO TO YOUR ROOM." He made a lunge towards Chrissie but Hannah intervened before she could stop herself.

"Don't you dare touch her!" Hannah yelled as she stepped in front of Chrissie. Dale just looked down at her and laughed. "How about you try and stop me," he said. "How could you? She's your daughter.." She looked across at her mum "And you're just going to let him? You're not going to do anything?"

 "We do a lot for you both, you'd think you'd both be a little more grateful," said Leanne. Hannah looked at her mum in disbelief. Her statement was not only completely untrue, it hit a nerve. "You do a lot for us!? Is that a joke? You've given us a bed to sleep in and a crumby roof over our heads but that's pretty much it. I'll be more grateful when you're both gone, that'll be the day."

 Chrissie gasped. "Daddy, I'm sorry," she said again, pleadingly. "Chrissie just go to your room…as for you," said Dale as he approached Hannah. Hannah rushed to the door before he could take another step. "Screw this, I'm out of here," she said and she slammed the door.

Hannah could feel her heart racing and her whole body shook with anger. The guilt penetrated her mind as she thought of Chrissie still in the house. But she didn't have a choice. She simply couldn't go back there. Not tonight. Not with both of them in that state. She could only hope that they would send Chrissie to her room and leave her there. Surely Dale wouldn't lay a hand on his little princess, he never had before.

Hannah made her move and headed to Tess's meeting point before Dale could follow. As she reached the park she sat on the slide and contemplated her situation. What would her next move be? She was thankful that she'd packed quickly and had brought a change of clothes. She would definitely be staying at Tess's.

Amanda

Amanda sat at the dinner table as Tyler struggled to take a breath, filling them in on the day's activities. Amanda tried her best to listen as he sat proudly, commenting on how impressed his friends had been that he'd shown up for school after such a heavy knock. Though she tried, she couldn't help thinking about Chrissie and wondering what she should do. She somehow felt guilty about calling her parents and hoped that Chrissie was ok.

"Mandy? Honey, Tyler asked you a question, what do you think?"

Amanda snapped out of her daze and starred at Danny, without any clue what Tyler had said. "Um, yeah, sure," she responded, hopefully. "Did you hear anything I said?" asked Tyler. "Well, yes, you were saying how supportive your friends were today."

Tyler looked at her, clearly unimpressed. "That was like forever ago mum, get with it."

"I'm sorry Ty, my mind's somewhere else today, what did you ask?"

"Forget it," he said and finally took a bite of his dinner. Danny looked at her, concerned. "Everything ok, honey?" She smiled. "Everything's fine, I just had a big day."

They sat in silence throughout dinner and Amanda couldn't help but feel like she'd let Tyler down. She needed to get what she was feeling off her chest and she followed Danny to the kitchen to clean up.

"I'm worried about one of the kids at school," she said, straight to the point. "Ok, what's up?" "Well, she said she wasn't feeling well and I phoned home, but her parents weren't too happy that I'd called."

Danny nodded but said nothing. He just stood in anticipation, waiting for more. When Amanda didn't say anything else he raised his eyebrows. "Ok, so her parents weren't happy... but you know what these kids' families are like. They don't care. I don't get it Mandy, what's the big deal?" Amanda sighed. "Something didn't feel right. I'm worried about her."

"Look, they were probably at home, being deadbeats like the majority of those parents and you woke them up. That's probably it. I think you're dramatizing the whole thing."
Amanda said nothing, she felt defeated. "You're probably right," she said and left him to clean the dishes.
Was Danny right? Was she just being paranoid? Maybe Chrissie would turn up to school tomorrow, good as gold and everything would be absolutely fine. That's when she made a decision. If something still didn't seem right tomorrow she would investigate further. Until then, she would give it a rest.

Hannah

Tess spotted Hannah sitting on the edge of the slide and she made her way over, accompanied by Jack and her older brother Max. They all had cigarettes in hand as Tess approached Hannah. "Hey,"
"Hey Han, glad you could make it," Tess eyed the backpack and pillow that was stuffed inside unsuccessfully. Hannah felt uneasy. "The pillow was just in case, I mean, I don't have to stay, I just.."
"No problem Han, of course you can stay. Jack is" she said and smiled. Hannah couldn't help but feel Max starring at her. The last thing she wanted was for him to make a move. "Come on then, let's get out of here."

They arrived at Tess's house and Hannah was reminded instantly of her own. Shabby, run down, dirty and with a foul smell that seemed to penetrate through the entire house. "You can sleep on the couch if you like, I doubt you'll want to be in my room tonight," said Tess as she wrapped her arms around Jack. "My room's free," said Max. Tess laughed. "In your dreams! Anyway, our parents aren't around so we can do whatever we want." "Or whoever," sniggered Max.
Hannah chose to ignore him and she made herself comfortable on the couch. Tess and Jack disappeared to the kitchen and Max

joined Hannah in front of the TV. He pulled out a powdery substance and emptied it onto the coffee table. Hannah looked at it with content. Was there any escaping that horrible stuff?
"Wanna try some Hannah? I'll let you have a sniff for free."
 Hannah didn't say anything, she simply looked at Max with disgust, indicating that she would *not* like to have a sniff. Hearing the conversation, Tess and Jack entered the room and spotted the white powder. "Where did you get that!?" Tess asked excitedly.
"Never you mind, you're not having any."
"Bullshit, give us some."
"No way."
"I'm pretty sure you offered Hannah some, why can't I have some?"
"Because then Jack will want some and there'll be none left."
"Oh come on, you can split that 4 ways, easy."
"Try 3 ways, I'm not touching it," said Hannah.
"Oh come off it Han, he'll give you some he's just being an idiot."
"I don't want any."
Tess just starred at Hannah, clearly unable to believe what she was hearing.
Hannah said no more, she jumped up off the couch and headed out the back. Tess was clearly too interested in her brother's drugs as she ignored Hannah and continued to plead for her fair share.

Hannah sighed to herself. Her situation now wasn't much of an improvement. They would all be stoned off their faces soon and she'd be back to square one. Maybe she should just join them. What harm could it do, really? Send her into insane stupidity like her mum? That seemed like a fair amount of harm.
On the other hand, if she had some maybe she'd forget about everything. Dale, her mum, her sister. Hannah couldn't bear to think about her sister and the fact that she'd left her at home. With that thought in mind she headed back inside.

The three of them were all kneeling down in front of the coffee table. Clearly Max had given in and was now sharing his stash. He didn't really seem to mind though, as the three of them sat laughing hysterically as Jack attempted to get his pile in a straight line. They didn't even notice Hannah as she stood watching them, contemplating what to do. Deep down she knew they weren't the answer, but she longed for a moment free from her thoughts, and the temptation was suddenly too great. She sat down next to Tess as she absorbed the remaining powder. "Got any left?" she asked hopefully. "Nope, you missed your chance Hannah Banana! Maybe next time," said Tess. "I can get more tomorrow if you really want Han, but you have to promise not to chicken out." "Deal," said Hannah, though she wasn't entirely sure. Jack grabbed Tess's hand and they headed to Tess's bedroom.

Hannah was the only sober one in the house, something she should be used to by now. "So, how about you and me head for my bedroom then?" said Max as he moved closer to Hannah. "No thanks," she replied. "Oh c'mon, we don't have to do anything, we can just talk, or whatever." Hannah knew better than to believe him, but she wasn't exactly sure how she could avoid him for the rest of the night. "I've got to go to the bathroom," she said and got to her feet.
It was only a temporary solution, but it would give her time to think.

The time passed by and Hannah could feel herself getting hungry. Maybe Max would be in a different frame of mind by now. She opened the door and headed for the kitchen. Max was nowhere to be seen so she opened the cupboard, hoping to find something substantial. The cupboards were practically bare which didn't really surprise her. She spotted a packet of chips and decided that they would have to do.
"Ohh yum, give me some!" said Max as he jumped up beside Hannah, causing her to drop the packet onto the floor. "Haha, some-

one's clumsy!" said Max as he attempted to pick up the chips. Hannah could tell that the drugs were taking effect. She bent down and snatched the chips as Max stumbled around, unable to balance himself. She sidestepped him and headed back to the couch, where she flung herself once again in front of the TV. Max followed her and sat down next to her. "Yum," he said again, but he wasn't looking at the chips, he was staring at Hannah's chest. He crawled along the couch and attempted to get on top of Hannah, but she pushed him away. "Get lost," she said.
"Oo, someone's feisty," he said and made another attempt towards Hannah, this time putting his arm around her waist. "I said get lost!" and she shoved him hard, hard enough that he fell back and hit his back against the coffee table. "Hey what gives? You fucking frigid or what?" asked Max aggressively as he tried to get up onto his feet. "I'm not interested. How about you get that through your head?" replied Hannah. She could feel her heart beating fast. Was she really going through this again? And with her best friend's brother?

She got up off the couch and headed for Tess's bedroom. She banged loudly on the door but there was no response. She really didn't want to barge in on them when she knew what they were doing. "Hey Tess, get out here. You're brother's being disgusting," she said.

She waited but nothing happened, until she felt two hands grasp onto her shoulders. "Stop playing hard to get," Max said. Hannah felt the anger rise up inside her and she elbowed him in the ribs. She turned around and shoved Max away from her. His coordination was virtually non-existent and she shoved him harder than she anticipated. He slammed into the wall with a thud that shook the house. The adrenalin inside Hannah took over and she felt her right hand form into a fist. "I *said* I'M NOT INTERESTED," but before she could take a swing, Tess's door burst open. "What is going on?!" asked Tess. "Why don't you ask your brother?" said Hannah as she took a breath. Tess looked across at Max who seemed disoriented. Tess appeared to be thinking things over and she stepped back inside her bedroom. She was saying something to Jack. A few seconds passed and then Jack appeared at the doorway. "Let's go get some food hey, Max. Maccas sound good?" said Jack. "Great idea!" said Max and he followed Jack down the hallway. Tess reappeared at the doorway. "You really think it's a good idea for Jack to be driving right now?" asked Hannah. Tess shrugged. "He does it all the time." "Right" Said Hannah. "So is your brother going to continue to be feral when he gets back?" Hannah asked. "He's always a bit crazy when he's high, he'll calm down."

"I don't know, he seemed pretty keen before he had any."

"Well yeah, he's always had a thing for you, Han. You're honestly not into him at all?"

"Are you out of your mind!?"

"Actually, yeah, a little bit," said Tess with a grin.

The boys returned with cheeseburgers and fries and Hannah could feel her mouth watering. She momentarily forgot about Max's advances as she dug into her burger. Nothing had ever tasted so good. They all appeared to be on their way down and Hannah eased up a little. She longed to give Chrissie a bite of her burger and some fries, it had been ages since they'd had fast food together.

Hannah was getting tired now and she lay herself down on the couch. Tess gave her a blanket and she and Jack once again headed for Tess's bedroom. Max must have already gone to bed. *Thank God,* thought Hannah as she settled her head down on her pillow.
Just as Hannah felt herself drifting off to sleep, she felt a large weight on top of her and heavy breathing. "What the!?" cried Hannah.
"Just shh, alright, I promise you, you'll be wondering why you

ever pushed me away."

"Get off me!" said Hannah and she tried to shove him off, but he was much stronger on top of her and he used his weight to force her to stay down. She had no other choice but to scream. She would only have one chance before he would place his hand over her mouth. "HELLLLLP!" she bellowed and she prayed that it had done the trick.

Tess and Jack ran out of the bedroom and this time Jack came to the rescue. "Hey, what are you doing!?" he said and pushed Max off Hannah. "She knows she wants me," said Max. "I don't think she does," said Jack. The two of them stood pushing and shoving and Tess grabbed Hannah's hand, leading her away to the bedroom. "I'm so sorry, Han. Do you want to go home?" she asked.

Hannah didn't know what she wanted. She couldn't even go to her friend's house and feel safe.

She wanted to escape to a different place, a different universe. Maybe one where she was with her real dad, in a place where he wouldn't hurt her or abuse or. Did such a person or place even exist?

Once again the tears built up in Hannah's eyes.

"I can't go home," she said hopelessly.

CHAPTER 6

Amanda

Amanda paid close attention to her students as they started trickling through the door, ready to start the new day. With each pupil who came inside, she became increasingly anxious. There was no sign of Chrissie yet. A knot inside the pit of Amanda's stomach grew as each minute passed. Where was she? The bell to signal start of class was not a good sign. Chrissie was never this late. Amanda couldn't think straight. Her uneasiness overwhelmed her and she was in no mood to teach. She made her way to the staff cupboard in search of a DVD. She scanned the back of each DVD, reading the running time of each one. It was only Tuesday, DVDs were more of a Friday afternoon thing, but she couldn't concentrate. She needed the time to think. She grabbed the latest Disney hit and wacked it in the DVD player. She could sense her students' excitement at the prospect of watching a movie on a Tuesday morning. She gave a guilty smile to herself and hoped Jenny, the Principal wouldn't be popping in for a visit this morning.

The movie was a slight help. She had seen it with Jenna 100 times so didn't feel the need to listen. Instead the thoughts inside her head played repeatedly as she tried to assure herself that Chrissie's absence was nothing to worry about. Maybe she really did have a stomach ache and her parents had kept her home. That made sense, didn't it? But why did they hang up on her? Why were they so aggressive? Why was something telling her that something was totally wrong?

And then she decided. She would drive past Chrissie's house after school. She wouldn't do anything, simply drive by and see if she could see any warning signs. Was that ridiculous? She didn't care. She got up off her chair and again searched for her students' contact details. She found Chrissie's address. As expected, she was on the 'wrong' side of the main road. Yet only 10 minutes from Amanda's house. Easy. She scribbled the address down on a sticky note and placed it in her handbag.

Danny would think it was ridiculous. Oh well, he didn't have to know. She needed answers and a simple sticky beak at the house might tell her everything she needed to know. She stepped back inside the classroom as the kids began singing along to the movie. She took a deep breath and smiled at the irony. One thing was for certain, Amanda could not let it go.

The rest of the day seemed to go backwards as Amanda counted down the clock. It was nearly the end of lunch and she'd sat in her office playing out the evening's possibilities in her head. As she ran through each scenario they became more and more extreme. The probability was that she would drive past and find absolutely nothing. She took a bite of her sandwich and noticed a pile of work on her desk. She'd moved it aside to write down Chrissie's address. She groaned to herself as she realised what the pile of work was. The latest assignment she'd given her students. She had promised to mark them and return them to her students by…Wednesday. Shit, that was tomorrow! Crap, crap, crap. She couldn't sit them through another DVD as she marked them. She should have marked them in the morning when she had the chance. But they had not been a priority. Was she taking this too far? She would have to mark them after class, then do her drive by. It meant Jenna and Tyler would be home by themselves for a couple of hours. She wasn't worried about Ty, but it wasn't his responsibility to look after Jenna. Wait, it was Tuesday. Danny would be home earlier to take Ty to football training. Jenna would just have to go too. She grabbed her phone and sent her husband a text. "Be home late, last minute mark-

ing. Please take Jenna with you tonight. Xo"
Done. That problem was solved. Plus it bought her some time to have a good look at Chrissie's house.
Before she made her decision, Amanda decided to phone Chrissie's house and see how her parents would react when she questioned their daughter's absence. It appeared she wouldn't find out. There was no answer, the phone simply rang out. This did nothing to reassure Amanda. Her mind was well and truly made up.

Hannah

Hannah slept on the floor in Tess's room. It hadn't been ideal but she simply couldn't go home and she felt too vulnerable on Tess's couch. At least Tess and Jack had respected her presence and had gone straight to sleep. The same couldn't be said for Hannah. She was cold, uncomfortable and her brain was full of unwanted thoughts. Not a good combination. Plus, she wanted to wake before anyone else and head straight to school on her own. Going to school was simply a no-brainer. She expected Max, Tess and Jack to take the day off and she felt like avoiding them all. She didn't need Max pestering her to keep to her word and take his drugs, and she didn't need Tess's questions. She just wanted to be alone. The only problem with this was when she was alone, she was alone with her thoughts and that was no good either.
Hannah got to her knees and peered up at the clock next to Tess's head. 7.45am. Finally.
She grabbed her backpack and pillow and made her way to the bathroom. She had the world's quickest shower, put on her change of clothes, ran her fingers through her hair and made her way to school.

Hannah did her best to concentrate in class, if anything it was a way to distract herself from her thoughts. But nothing she read would stay inside her head. The words made no sense and she felt her stomach rumbling. She was used to not having breakfast, but something else was going on inside. She felt uneasy. She shouldn't have left Chrissie alone. What had she been thinking? She had been totally selfish and she hated herself for it. But her instincts had told her to flee, to get as far from the house as possible. At the time, she hadn't had a choice. She simply had to get out of there. But now she was filled with a sense of regret. She kept telling herself her sister was fine, that they wouldn't do anything to her, not to their precious little angel.

"Hannah," her teacher was addressing her now. '*Here we go*,' thought Hannah. English was not her strong suit and Shakespeare's plays were definitely going to do her no favours. "What is your opinion on this scene? Do you think Juliette should have ended her life so quickly? Or do you think love made the decision a simple one for her?" Hannah stared blankly back. She didn't have a clue. "Well…" her teacher pushed. An answer was better than nothing, Hannah figured. "Well, I think she made the right decision. If she had the guts to end her life, then good on her. If I had the guts, I'd do it too."

She didn't know where it came from, but she couldn't help but feel like it was a truthful answer. Her teacher didn't appear to appreciate her honesty. "That is not at all appropriate Hannah. I am getting a little tired of your lack of respect in this class. You can spend detention with me after school."

Hannah said nothing. What was the point? She couldn't believe what had happened. It was so unfair. If anything, Hannah had expected her teacher to find her answer to be somewhat alarming and perhaps a welfare issue, yet she had given her detention. Was she ever going to catch a break?

Hannah's slight break came when detention only lasted 15 minutes. The rain was falling hard outside, pounding loudly on the windows and Hannah's teacher had let everyone go early. Hannah was almost waiting for her to say 'except you Hannah, you can wait', but when she said nothing, Hannah jumped up and raced out the door. If she hurried she would make it to Chrissie's class on time.

Her backpack and pillow were soaked, but she didn't care. She had made it right as the bell sounded. She puffed and panted and knelt next to the gate to catch her breath. Chrissie's teacher spotted her and made her way over. Hannah rolled her eyes automatically.

"Hannah, what are you doing here?"
"What do you think? I'm picking up my sister."
"Chrissie didn't come to school today," said Amanda. Hannah thought quickly, realising it must look strange that she didn't know this.
"Oh, that's right. I remember now, silly me," she turned to leave.
"Wait a minute. Is she ok?"
"None of your business," Hannah responded aggressively. Panic was rising inside her and she didn't need Chrissie's nosey teacher making things worse.
"Actually, it is my business. She's my pupil and I have a duty of care."
"And I have a duty of care to keep people out of other people's business. Bye," said Hannah and she stormed off.
Why hadn't Chrissie gone to school? Was she hurt? What had they done to her? Why oh, why had she left her there, with them, unsafe and unprotected?
The guilt swarmed over Hannah and she hurried home.

The rain came heavy and fast now and she could feel her socks getting drenched as she raced through the puddles. There was no time to bother sidestepping them.

She pulled into the street, the white picket fence gleaming in the grey, wet weather. There were no lights on and no sounds of the television blasting. Hannah went to open the door, but it was locked.

That was unusual. They never locked the door. Not if they were home. She peered through the window but there was no movement. The house was dark. She wiped her wet hair out of her face and looked around, when she spotted something big and rectangular outside the gate.

Hannah made her way to the shape, when suddenly she recognised the blue and white pattern.

Her mattress, along with her doona, had been ripped from her bed and dumped outside the house.

She peered down at it and then it came to her. They had effectively removed her bed to sleep in and the roof over her head. A hatred so deep built up inside her and she flung herself, her pillow and backpack onto the mattress, punching every inch of her mattress until she was out of breath and exhausted.

Hannah lay there as the rain pelted down. She was completely drenched and freezing to the core. She sat up and hugged her pillow tight. Where was she supposed to go now? She couldn't go back to Tess's and she couldn't get inside the house. Maybe she should break a window and climb inside. But she didn't want to go inside that place, and what would they do to her if they came back and realised she'd damaged the house? The tears began to seep from her eyes, blending in with the rain that continued to fall. As she squeezed her pillow she felt something rough against her cheek. She reached into the pillow case and pulled out the cookie wrapper she had kept from Chrissie. She wiped her face and held the wrapper in her hands. The one thing in the world that kept her sane, made her feel loved. And they had taken it from her. She screamed in frustration and flung herself back onto her cold, wet bed. She buried her face in her hands, but the gleam from bright headlights caused her to lift her head.

Amanda

Amanda raced through her student's assignments. She had asked them to explore their backyard and draw pictures of plants, animals and insects that they found. She made a mental note to herself to look through them closer tomorrow as she flicked through and found some amusing 5-year-old drawings. But she had no time to look at them now. Instead she gave them all gold stars and placed them back on her desk.

She walked out the door but rushed back inside and grabbed her coat. She hadn't even noticed the rain in her efforts to get out as soon as possible. The rain was actually ridiculous. Hadn't it been sunny and hot only last week? *'Only in Melbourne,'* she thought as she rushed to the staff car park. She hopped into her car, grabbed Chrissie's address and keyed it in to her GPS. She took a deep breath and reminded herself to take it easy on the wet roads.

Amanda couldn't help but feel a little uneasy as she edged closer to Chrissie's street. The houses seemed to go from bad to worse as she drove past each one. She drove slowly as she eyed each letter box, looking for Chrissie's number. It was hard to see with the rain coming down heavy and the lack of street lights to guide her. She reached what she believed to be the right house when a strange sight caught her eye. What appeared to be a mattress was lying out the front. *'It wasn't rubbish collection week,'* Amanda thought to herself. She positioned her car so that her headlights shone over the mattress. There appeared to be a human shape on top of the mattress, along with doona and pillow. What on earth? 'What would someone be doing in this weather with their bed outside!? Did people seriously sleep on the street, only 10 minutes from her lush suburb?'

As Amanda's car drew closer the person on the bed began to move, and Amanda gasped as she recognised the face glaring across at her through the rain.

Hannah

Panic overtook Hannah as she attempted to identify the owner of the bright lights. Had they come back? Was Chrissie ok? But as her eyes began to adjust she came to realise that she didn't recognise what appeared to be a four wheel drive. Her brain attempted to process the image. Big, black, shiny, expensive. Definitely not familiar. 'Did they steal it?' she wondered. The car crept next to the curb so that it was parallel to the mattress, the headlights dimmed as the car was parked.
Hannah braced herself as the driver door opened. An umbrella was drawn and the unknown driver stepped out of the car and made their way around the back towards Hannah underneath the umbrella. Hannah was still holding her pillow and she squeezed it against her. It certainly wasn't going to help her much but it gave her a small sense of protection.
As the driver approached she knelt down beside Hannah and lifted her umbrella enough so that Hannah could make out an outline of what seemed to be a female face.
"Hannah, what on earth are you doing here? What's happened?" Hannah recognised the voice she'd heard only hours before. She gasped and chucked her pillow aside. "What the hell?" she couldn't believe it. "Are you some kind of stalker?"
It was all Hannah could say as she comprehended the fact that her sister's teacher was now standing outside their house. "I told you, I have a duty of care and your sister…" "and I thought I told you to mind your own…" "Hannah, I think we can establish this is my business. Now it seems we both have a common goal here, so the choice is yours. You can stay here, freezing to death, alone and with no clue where your sister is. Or you can come with me and we can try and figure this out together." Hannah scoffed at her. "Are you serious? As if I'd go anywhere with you." "Suit yourself. Stay here, catch pneumonia. I'm sure Chrissie will be thrilled to know her sister sat out here, feeling sorry for herself, and did nothing at all to help her, or find her. If you're ok

with that Hannah, I'll go."

Hannah just glared at her. She knew what she was doing, and she wanted to be smarter, and even tell her where to go. Chrissie's teacher made her way back to her car and opened the driver door. She seemed to wait momentarily before she hopped in, as if hoping Hannah might jump up and tell her to stop. Hannah's mind raced. What *would* Chrissie think? She seemed to like this manipulative teacher of hers. Maybe Hannah could trust her. If Hannah didn't do something, she might never know what Chrissie would think. That thought seemed to make up Hannah's mind. She jumped up and opened the passenger door as the car's engine began to run. "Wait," she said.

CHAPTER 7

Amanda

The afternoon's drive by proceedings had certainly not gone to plan as Chrissie's drenched sister took a seat inside Amanda's Range Rover. She had to smile at the shock on Hannah's face when she realised her seat warmed beneath her. Amanda wished she had a towel to relieve Hannah of the awful, soaked feeling, but she had bigger things to worry about. Like 1, what Danny and the kids would say when she returned home with a soggy teenager. She would figure that out later. Instead she began to ask Hannah questions to gain an idea of where her sister might be. She wanted to ask what on earth had caused her to be outside in the rain on what was no doubt her own mattress. But for now, finding Chrissie was priority number one.

 As it turned out though, Hannah was being far from helpful. "So, has this happened before?" Silence. "Hannah, is your sister ok? Did you do something to upset them? Did Chrissie do something?"
Each question was unanswered. Hannah just stared out the window as if Amanda wasn't there. Amanda kept trying. "Is this out of character? Are you worried? You must be worried. I know I am. And don't say it's not my business…" she thought maybe that would hit a nerve, but still nothing. "What does your mum, LEanne do? And your dad, Dale what does…" "He's *not* my dad." Hannah said suddenly. '*Bingo,*' thought Amanda. She'd found that nerve and smacked it on the head.
"Oh, he's not? But he's Chrissie's dad?" Amanda continued. Han-

nah didn't say anything, but she gave a small nod. Amanda was getting somewhere. "Where is your dad?" Hannah shrugged her shoulders. "Have you ever met him?" Hannah shook her head. "Have you ever wanted to find him?" she shrugged her shoulders again. "Maybe you should try and find him, track him down," the charades ended as Hannah responded. "One missing person at a time, thanks," she said with a tiny trace of charisma in her voice. Amanda hadn't heard that before. She smiled to herself. There was life inside this girl somewhere and on top of finding Christina, Amanda had a new mission. She would help bring more of that life outside of Hannah.

Hannah

Hannah had done her best to ignore Chrissie's teacher for the entire trip. She was uneasy and didn't know what to expect or where exactly she was going. She glared at the rain outside as her body began to heat up inside the warmth of the car. Now, she was again thinking of her father, imagining him driving the car and taking her somewhere safe, away from everything. "I'm Amanda by the way, I don't think I've properly introduced myself."
 Hannah's thoughts were again interrupted by Chrissie's teacher. She didn't say anything back, she hated small talk, but Chrissie's teacher – Amanda, seemed to love it.

They pulled into a large driveway and Hannah glanced up at the house. It was enormous. Amanda pressed a button and the garage door began to open. "Ah, still at footy training. Danny is my husband. Cameron is my eldest, but he doesn't live at home anymore. I figured you could sleep in his room. And there's Tyler, he's probably about your age, and then there's Jenna, same age as Chrissie."

Hannah took a moment to take it all in. 3 kids in a house larger than anything Hannah had ever laid eyes on. And only 2 of them were at home. What the hell did they use it all for!?

They stepped inside and Hannah took a moment to look around. The house was immaculate, spotless, clean and fresh. "Come on, I'll show you to Cameron's room so you can get settled. And I'm sure Tyler has something you can borrow for the night. You must be freezing in those saturated clothes!" Amanda led Hannah up the stairs.

Upstairs was just as gigantic. There was a big lounge room filled with an oversized TV, 3 bedrooms and a bathroom. Amanda showed Hannah to the third bedroom, which had been transformed into a spare room. Hannah gasped as she spotted the ensuite next to the walk in robe. "Cam's room. Make yourself comfortable, I'll just go grab you some clothes."

Hannah dropped her backpack and pillow onto the floor. They looked completely out of place rugged and wet next to what had to be a King Size bed. Hannah didn't know what to think. She hadn't been expecting anything like this. She cringed at what Amanda must have thought when she's spotted Hannah on her mattress outside her dump of a house. *'Thank God she didn't see the inside,'* Hannah thought to herself.

Amanda returned with tracksuit pants, t-shirt and jumper. "Tyler won't mind if you wear these. I'll leave you be while you get changed. Bring me all your wet clothes when you're done, I'll be downstairs. I've been a bit rushed tonight so I'm going to whip up some spaghetti. I hope you like it." Hannah just nodded, she was completely speechless, this time unintentionally.

Hannah changed into Tyler's clothes. She felt awkward wearing some stranger's clothes, particularly when she'd no doubt be meeting that stranger later. The thought made her a little uncomfortable. What was she doing here? She stuffed her saturated dress into her backpack and took it with her downstairs. She followed the smell of food to the kitchen which was also oversized.

"Ah, that's better," said Amanda as she looked over Hannah in

her new attire. She grabbed Hannah's backpack and exited the room. In Amanda's momentary absence, Hannah took herself on a tour around the lounge room.
There were photos everywhere of Amanda's family. The smiling, happy faces looked back at Hannah and she felt increasingly out of place.

Amanda pulled a chair for Hannah and placed a bowl of spaghetti in front of it. "Take a seat Hannah, you might as well have yours now. No point waiting for the others and letting it get cold!"

A part of Hannah wanted to leave. She couldn't explain why, she just didn't feel right. As much as she had an urge to run out the door, the smell of hot spaghetti was enough to sway her and she took her seat at the table. "The clan should be home soon. They aren't exactly expecting company, but not to worry."

Hannah could hear the small hint of anxiety in Amanda's voice, which didn't make her feel any better. Thankfully, the spaghetti was proving to be a good distraction. It was better than anything Hannah had ever tasted and she scoffed it down in record timing.

She wondered what the rest of the family would all say when they spotted the skinny, untidy, scrawny teenager sitting at their sparkly dinner table. Hannah didn't know if she could handle the looks of disapproval she would no doubt receive. "Thanks for dinner," she said as she made her way to the sink to clean her dish. "Here," said Amanda as she took the bowl and placed it in the dishwasher. "Would you like dessert? We've got ice cream?"

Hannah didn't want to stick around. She wanted to escape before the others got home. "I think I might go to bed, I'm tired," she said. She felt exhausted and she couldn't think straight. She didn't have the energy to worry about Chrissie any longer. Amanda glanced at the clock but seemed to approve of Hannah's early night. "Ok. I guess we can figure out what to do about Chrissie tomorrow. You've had a rough day. Yell out if you need anything."

"Thanks."

Hannah made her way up the stairs. As she reached the top she heard a large sound as the garage door lifted. *'Good timing,'* she thought to herself. A scramble at the door and voices echoed up through the stairs. "What's for dinner? I'm starving!"

Hannah waited at the top as she heard Amanda speaking from the kitchen. "Pipe down, we've got spaghetti and a… err, special guest with us, so keep your voices down." Hannah gulped. "Sounds great honey, Jenna put your toys away would you, and what's this about a guest?"

Hannah had to strain her ears to hear. "Well, just for tonight, really. It's, well. It shouldn't be a problem, she's already upstairs in bed."

"Who?"

"Hannah"

"Who's Hannah?"

"Chrissie, my student I was telling you about. Her sister."

"Right… and why is your student's sister staying with us?"

"Because she needed somewhere to stay, and I offered and well, now she's here."

Amanda had side stepped the 'Chrissie is missing and I found her sister outside her house on her mattress' part. Hannah was grateful for that, but Danny clearly didn't approve. "How old is she?"

"Um, about Tyler's age. 15 or so,"

"What?" Tyler muffled through a mouthful of pasta, but he was ignored.

"Honey, do you really think that's appropriate?"

"What? It's just one night, Danny come on, be reasonable, it will be fine." A moment's silence. Perhaps he was contemplating it, perhaps Amanda was batting her eyelids. "Fine, one night," he said as the sound of a chair against floorboards creaked. They had apparently all huddled in to their dinner.

'*I guess that's settled then,*' Hannah thought as she made her way to her temporary bedroom. She got undressed and prepared the shower. The water heated instantly and Hannah jumped straight in. The shower had a full supply of shampoo, conditioner and body wash so she grabbed the shampoo bottle and ran the lotion through her hair. It certainly wasn't the type of shower she was used to. At home, the water was barely warm and her cheap shampoo made her hair frizz.

As she jumped out of the shower and towel-dried her hair, she thought about her sister and what she was doing. The guilt once again consumed her as she put Tyler's clothes back on. She couldn't help but feel that being here wasn't helping Chrissie any more than being on her own mattress in the cold, but she couldn't think any longer. She jumped into the mega-sized bed and drifted off to sleep.

Hannah was still half asleep when she stumbled out of bed the next morning. Surprisingly, she'd had a really good sleep despite yesterday's events. She stepped out of the room and collided with a fast moving object that reached up to her waist. "Watch where you're going!" the object spoke. It was Jenna, Amanda's daughter. "Oops, I thought you were my brother, sorry." "I guess I am wearing his clothes," said Hannah apologetically. "Yeah, totally confused me," she laughed. "My name is Jenna. Who are you?" She was abrupt and full of confidence. Hannah was a little taken aback. "Er, I'm Hannah," she said. "Are you Tyler's girlfriend?" she asked.

Hannah hoped Danny hadn't heard her, she couldn't imagine that going down too well. "Oh, no I'm not, I'm… um… your mum's…friend." She didn't know how to explain. "I'm one of your mum's student's sisters," she added, finding it a little amusing that she was explaining herself to a 6 year old. "Is your sister here too?" Jenna asked hopefully. "No, she's not."

Hannah was again forced to think of her sister. She wished she could stop feeling guilty every time she thought about her.
Jenna made her way down the stairs and Hannah contemplated following her. She would have to meet the rest of the 'clan' sooner or later.
"Nice clothes," a voice from behind her made her jump. She turned around to see a teenage boy peering over at her across his bedroom doorway. "No offence, but I think they look better on me." He had the same confidence about him as his sister. "I bet," was all Hannah could manage. "So, you must be Hannah? I'm Tyler. I'm not really sure why you're here but as long as I get those clothes back I don't really care," he winked at Hannah and she smiled back. "Anyway, I'm starving, are you here for breakfast?" Hannah shrugged. "I take that as a yes, you look like you could do with some." He looked her up and down. He was fit and healthy and she looked like a stick in comparison.
Hannah was silent. Tyler seemed to lose interest and followed his nose down the stairs. Hannah could hear them all talking happily over breakfast. If she hadn't been wearing Tyler's clothes she would have contemplated running out the door.

Hannah took a deep breath and made her way into the kitchen. She didn't even want breakfast, she just wanted her dress and her backpack and then she could leave. "Just in time for bacon and eggs!" said Amanda enthusiastically as she spotted Hannah. "I'm not hungry."

Danny glanced up at her above his newspaper. "Mandy's gone

to a lot of trouble. The least you could do is have a bite to eat." Hannah was familiar with the direct tone. She glared back at him. She hadn't asked for a fancy breakfast. "I just want my clothes and my bag," Danny began to reply, but Amanda interrupted. "Sure, they're over there by the door. Well, your dress is on the door."

Hannah looked across in the direction Amanda was pointing. Her dress had been washed, dried and ironed and was hanging on a coat hanger on the door knob. She hadn't asked for that either. She hadn't asked for anything.
"Are you sure you don't want any breakfast? I can make toast if you just want toast?"
"I'm fine" said Hannah and she grabbed her dress off the coat hanger.
"Not even a thank you?" Danny probed. Hannah stared back at him, she could feel the temper rising inside her. "Thanks *Mandy*," she said a little too sarcastically. She wasn't exactly sure what was bothering her. Danny didn't say anything, he just raised his eyebrows at Amanda as if to ask if she was serious.
Hannah grabbed her backpack and raced up the stairs. She changed as quickly as possible and made her way back down. She didn't even say goodbye, she just opened the front door and left. As she stepped onto the porch she realised one small problem. She had no idea how to get to school, or home, or anywhere for that matter. Jenna followed her out with soccer ball in hand, not bothering to close the door behind her. "Are you going to school?" Jenna asked conversationally as she began kicking her ball against the side of the fence. "If I can figure out how to get there," Hannah replied.
"What school do you go to?"
"Heanwood"
"My mum teaches there! I have no idea where that is, but mum can probably drop you off, she drops me off." "I bet she does" said Hannah.
Jenna just looked at her, a little puzzled and clearly not under-

standing what Hannah meant. Hannah watched Jenna as she continued to kick her ball. She was totally off balance and her loose laces were preventing her from getting any real control over the ball. "Why don't you tie your laces up?" Hannah asked, she was getting frustrated watching her shoe nearly slip every time her foot connected with the ball. Jenna bent down and began to tie up her shoe. Hannah stood and watched as she tried and tried to do up her laces. Hannah smiled to herself. The girl with everything couldn't tie her own shoelaces. "Here," said Hannah and she knelt down to assist. "Watch, one bunny ear, two bunny ears, loop them together and what do you get, a tied up shoe, don't forget!" Jenna watched in awe as Hannah successfully tied her laces together. "I've never been shown that way before!" said Jenna excitedly. "Now you try," said Hannah as she untied them. Jenna began to re-attempt her laces, determined to get them right.

Hannah had taught Chrissie the same riddle, her sister had grasped it almost instantly and had paraded around the house, proudly showing off her pair of bunny ears.

As Hannah reminisced, Amanda appeared at the doorway. "Jenna, please go back inside and get ready for school."

"Look mummy, look at my laces!"

"That's great Jen, now please get back inside, I need to drop Hannah off." She looked at Hannah.

"School or home?" she asked. "I just want to find my sister."

"Yes, and I'm trying to help you do that. Would you prefer to go home or school?"

"What makes you think she'd be at either?"

"Well, where do *you* think she is?"

"I don't know"

"Right. Well in that case I think we should go to one of the two places we know of that she might be."

"What do you mean 'we'?" Hannah asked.

"For god's sake Hannah, are we seriously going through this again? She's my pupil, I'd like to find her too."

Hannah said nothing. She didn't want anyone's help. She didn't *need* anyone's help.

"Look, I know you've got a lot on your mind"

"No, you don't. You don't know anything about me."

"I know you've got a younger sister that you care about a lot, I know that you're concerned about her, you look out for her, you're worried that she's in the care of people that aren't very capable of looking after her. Namely her father who you really disapprove of. I know you feel lost, tired, frustrated and upset and you really don't want to hang out with your sister's teacher. You also don't know how to get to school, or home, and you're angry about that too. Your only way of finding your sister is to jump in her annoying teacher's car and start looking. So what will it be? School or home?" She finally took a breath and Hannah simply glared at her. She didn't want to admit it to herself, but she had just summed up her emotions in 10 seconds flat.

"School" she said, defeated.

CHAPTER 8

Amanda

The last 18 hours had been full of surprises for Amanda. For one, she certainly hadn't expected to find Chrissie's sister drenched from head to toe on her mattress as she'd approached her house. She'd been completely shocked that the bordering-on-anorexic girl had refused a bowl of ice cream after she'd scoffed her dinner in record timing. And while she could understand her attitude, she had been a little taken aback at the lack of appreciation for the trouble Amanda had gone to, not to mention the fact that her house must have seemed like a palace in comparison, yet there had been no sign at all of any admiration from Hannah. Amanda's vanity was a little shameful, but she simply couldn't believe it. On top of that, Hannah had completely surprised her by electing to go to school rather than home. *'Things at her house must be terrible,'* Amanda thought to herself. It wasn't a good sign.

Amanda pulled up outside Liberty Park as she dropped Tyler and Jenna off to school. She couldn't help but hear Hannah snort under her breath which happened to be the first sound she'd made since hopping into the car.

"Have a good day guys, I'll be waiting here tonight after work, I shouldn't be late."

"See you mum. See you… actually, will I see you again?" Tyler looked through the window at Hannah questioningly. "Unlikely," she muttered, more to herself than to him. Tyler shrugged his shoulders, picked up Jenna's backpack and headed for school.

"You don't think you'll see Tyler again? Was last night really that terrible?" Hannah said nothing, she just glared out the window with the same body language she'd had the night before. "With any luck, Chrissie will be in class today and everything will be fine." Amanda said reassuringly.

She pulled out of the curb and continued the drive to the next destination. Hannah remained silent and Amanda gave up the challenge of trying to get her to speak.

She arrived at Heanwood and entered the staff car park. "You can get out first if you don't want to be seen with me," Amanda offered. Hannah remained silent and stayed put. She couldn't work her out.

They both got out of the car together and made their way to the Prep classrooms. As they approached the classroom, Chrissie was sitting on the outside bench running her fingers through her hair. "Chrissie!" Hannah exclaimed and ran towards her. Amanda felt suddenly awkward. Should she give them some space? But she wanted to know what had happened, she had every right to know.

"Where were you? Are you ok?" asked Hannah as Amanda approached. "What do you mean, where was *I*? Mum said she told you we went to Uncle Phil's". Hannah stood back, clearly both angry and puzzled. "Why didn't you come too? Mum said you would meet us there." Hannah looked blank, like she was trying to concoct a story as to why she hadn't followed those plans. Amanda couldn't stop herself, she had to intervene, she needed answers. "Chrissie, do you know why Hannah's mattress was left outside in the rain?" Hannah got up now, facing Amanda with daggers in her eyes. Chrissie shrugged her shoulders. "I don't know, Daddy said Hannah would think it was funny, but I didn't really get it". Before Amanda could say or do anything else, Hannah grabbed Chrissie's arm and led her away. Amanda wanted to follow, but she was once again harassed by Cindy's mum.

By the time Amanda had freed herself, she had lost any hope of getting anything out of Chrissie. Hannah had clearly instructed her not to say anything. She was again struck with the same instinct that told her something was very wrong. Chrissie was not herself and Hannah had certainly not been pleased to learn that Chrissie had been at her uncles' house. She was at a loss as to what to. She raced after Hannah who had hugged Chrissie goodbye.

"Hannah, wait! You need to tell me what's going on." "No, I don't. Just stay out of it ok, leave us alone."

"Hannah, I know something's wrong, you shouldn't go back there tonight."

"Well, it's my home isn't it, I don't really have a choice." "Yes, you do, I can help."

"No, you can't. What am I meant to do? Take Chrissie and go live at yours? It doesn't work like that."

"No, not at mine. Hannah, you need to find your father."

"Don't you get it? He doesn't want to be found, does he? If he did he wouldn't have left. So just stay out of it."

"You don't know that. Don't you want to find out? I've got resources, I've got… things."

"No, you don't. You have a fancy house and a car that lights a fucking fire under your ass. Sorry, but none of that's much help to me." Amanda continued to press, eager to get through to her, eager to assist.

"I know people, people who help with this stuff. Hannah, for all you know your dad doesn't even know you exist. It's worth knowing. Surely it's better than the alternative? Here."

Amanda reached into her pocket and pulled out a sticky note and pen. She scribbled her number on the paper and handed it to Hannah. "Please, don't rip this up. Just hold onto it, in case you need it, in case you change your mind."

"Unlikely" Hannah said again, but to Amanda's relief, she stuffed the note into her pocket, still intact. "Ok well fine, I've done all I can do now Hannah, I won't ask any more questions.

To your or to Chrissie. It's in your hands now."

Amanda wasn't sure if she would stick to her word, but she had to try. She had to earn Hannah's trust, and if that meant leaving her and Chrissie alone for as long as she could handle, maybe Hannah would come to her.

Hannah

Hannah fiddled with the scrunched up sticky note in her pocket as she made her way to her locker. She was doubtful she'd ever even look at what was written on it, but she chose to leave it in her pocket. It kept her hand occupied at the very least.

She could feel the tension build up inside her, she felt her fingers tingling and knew all too well that they weren't numb from the cold.

She now had Uncle Phil to worry about. Another problem brought on by Dale. In fact, Phil was basically where all the mess had started. He'd introduced his baby brother to the drugs in the first place. 'What a fucking family, and they're not even *my* family,' she sighed to herself as she approached the locker bay. As she grabbed her things she was knocked forward by a friendly bump. "Yo, Hannah Banana! Wassup, where'd you disappear to yesterday!?" It was Tess, and she seemed strangely upbeat. "I.. came to school," Hannah couldn't think of anything off the top of her head, so she opted for the truth. "You came *here!?* Geez Hannah, do I even know you at all!? What gives, you should have hung round, things got pretty wild yesterday."

"I can imagine," replied Hannah tonelessly. "Well, you should totally come over tonight, Max is getting more, you can have some this time, and who knows, maybe the two of you can even get it on," she winked and nudged Hannah again.

"I thought I told you I wasn't interested."

"In Max or the other 'stuff?'"

"Both."

"Seriously Han, what is up with you? You've gone all… lameo."

Hannah could feel the frustration build up inside her now. Her only friend was being difficult and she couldn't be bothered with it.

"That stuff isn't good Tess. It messes you up. It messes everything up. I just can't be around it right now, or anyone else who's on it. So if that's what you want to do then fine, but count me out, ok?"

"Fine, your loss. See you later." Tess turned and walked away, leaving Hannah alone, feeling hurt and let down. Her only friend hadn't even sensed that she was off, that something might have happened, that maybe something had caused her to say those things. Nope, she was too self-absorbed and judging by her behaviour she was more than likely already under the influence. Hannah slammed her locker shut and gathered her things. She was in no mood to get to class. She leant against her locker as everyone else made their way to the next period.

Maybe she should have gone to Tess's. It would be a good way to escape from everything. But she couldn't. Chrissie needed her, and what good was she to her if she wasn't home, or wasn't in the right frame of mind? Hannah sometimes hated that she cared so much. Things would be a lot easier if she didn't.

Hannah spent the rest of the day slumped against a tree a few blocks from her school. Attending class would be a waste of time today. She knew she'd already had more than her fair share of days off, but she didn't really care. What was school going to do for her? Educate her on how to remove herself from her dropkick family and her run-down house? Unlikely.

Hannah's back began to ache and her stomach rumbled. She had missed lunch which was nothing new but it didn't stop her stomach from aching. She stretched out her legs and contemplated going for a walk. Maybe she could wait for Chrissie outside her classroom. She glanced at her watch. It was late enough that she could probably start making her way over.

Chrissie seemed in good spirits as she came from the classroom. Hannah had knelt down in front of the fence so that Amanda wouldn't spot her. She didn't need any more questions.
"Why are you crouched down like that?" asked Chrissie curiously. "I was… just doing my shoe lace," she peered down at her shoe which was inconveniently undone. "Well, you didn't do a very good job!" laughed Chrissie and she knelt down to tie it up. "The student becomes the master," said Hannah as Chrissie tied her laces. "Not bad at all, kiddo," she said, lifting her foot in the air and admiring her work. Hannah's spirits were automatically raised by Chrissie's presence. She was all that kept her going some days.
"What would I do without you?" she asked, putting her arm around Chrissie as they made their way back home. "Well, you'd be really sad, and you'd probably trip over a lot." Hannah had to laugh at her matter-of-fact response.

As the sisters turned into their street, Hannah's heart sank as she recognised the car parked out the front of their house. "Do you know why Uncle Phil is at our house?" she tried to sound casual. Chrissie shrugged her shoulders. "I don't know, why not?"
"It's just, well, you just saw him right? Why would he be back already?"
"Maybe he came to say hello to you."
Hannah knew that wasn't the case, but then, was it the reason? Had he decided to pay her a visit? She shuddered at the thought. He was completely repulsive.
Hannah began to lag as she weighed up her options. As she slowly inched closer, she noticed that her mattress was nowhere to be seen. Had they put it back inside? Had it been collected by the dump removal people? She didn't really want to find out. Yet her choices were limited. She would have to go back at some stage, she might as well get it over with. Besides, Chrissie wouldn't understand if she didn't return home and

then maybe she would start to catch on. Hannah didn't want to risk that.

Hannah opened the front door and heard voices in the kitchen. Her plan to grab a quick bite and head to her room was ruined, there was no way she'd be seeing Phil if she could help it. Her stomach groaned but she bypassed the kitchen and headed for her bedroom. She opened her door and dropped her bag. The smell of wet dog filled the room. It didn't take Hannah long to identify the damp smell's origin as she looked at her bed. Her mattress had been carelessly dumped on top of it and was completely soaked through. She'd be sleeping on the floor tonight. She hovered in the doorway, the sight of her bed made her eyes water. She blinked back the tears and tried to think straight. Maybe she could share her sister's bed. And promote more questions? Not happening. She took one step towards her bed when she sensed a large body behind her.

"Your bed's lookin' a bit worse for wear inn'it?" said Phil with a chuckle. Hannah felt herself cringe. He was blocking the doorway, trapping her inside her room. She didn't say anything.

"Perhaps you'd be more comfortable on the couch, you know, where I'm sleepin?" He was such a sleaze. "Over my dead body," she replied before she could stop herself. "Well, that can be arranged." The humour in his voice had been replaced by anger. Clearly he didn't appreciate her attitude.

Hannah turned around and faced her step uncle. He was larger than his brother in height and weight, yet Hannah knew his brain was much smaller. "I'd like to see you try," she said, sounding braver than she felt. "That right?" he said taking a step closer. As he lifted his left foot Hannah moved swiftly towards his right and escaped from her room. "You get back here, you rude little slut!" he shouted after her.

Hannah raced from the room but she didn't get very far. She ran straight into Dale as Phil followed close behind her. The strong scent of whiskey filled Hannah's nostrils and she gasped as she spotted the empty bottle in Dale's hand.

"What's gun'on?" Dale's speech was slurred and he blinked his eyes stupidly at Hannah. Phil was first to respond.

"Your misses must'a done it with some feral bastard, 'cause she's sure created a little piece of scum." The rage built up inside Hannah. "What, as opposed to the complete lowlife that gave birth to pathetic parasites, twice?"

Hannah didn't know why she didn't just shut her mouth, she should have known better. But they infuriated her so much and she had to stand up to them, even if it meant suffering the painful consequences.

She wasn't sure how she was going to get out of this one. Alcohol generally slowed Dale down but at the same time, it heightened his aggression. As for Phil, he was impeccably dumb but regretfully strong. She could definitely outsmart him, but there was no way she'd out muscle him, whether he was under the influence or not.

"I think this little scumbag needs another lesson. How about you teach her just how 'pathetic' we can be." Dale gestured to Phil and Hannah instinctively turned around, trying to see what sort of plan they were concocting. Before she could make sense of anything, Dale swung his fist and connected with Hannah's nose. Hannah knew he hadn't hit her with complete force, he was off balance and his vision was out of whack. Despite this, the impact was intense and it caused Hannah to stumble backwards. Her eyes stung and it felt as if her nose had been pushed inside out.

Hannah tried in vain to keep her feet. She knew if she didn't she was in trouble. Her efforts failed. Dale shoved her, knocking her off balance and causing her to fall to the ground. Her face was throbbing and she could hear them laughing, sniggering. "Still. Think. We're. parasites?" asked Phil, kicking her in the stomach in time with each word he spoke. "Can a parasite do this?" Dale stumbled over her, he had each leg on either side of her. He knelt down and raised the empty whiskey bottle above his head. Hannah raised her hands to protect her face, leaving her stomach vulnerable. She could barely breathe as Phil continued to attack her.

She closed her eyes and braced herself. The hit never came. Instead, a tiny, quivering voice could be heard from the doorway. "Daddy?" Hannah opened her eyes and lifted her head towards the sound. There was her sister standing in the door way, utterly petrified. Hannah peered up at Dale. He hadn't managed to remove the evil, monstrous look from his eyes, the look he usually saved just for her. "Chrissie, we were just playing around. Don't be scared now sweetie, it's not real blood, it's not." In an instant, Chrissie bolted. Hannah blinked and she was gone.

Dale chucked the whiskey bottle aside and stumbled after her, motioning for Phil to follow.

Hannah attempted to catch her breath. Her abs ached and as she touched her nose she realised it was bleeding. So that was what Dale had meant by the blood. Poor Chrissie. Her world had just been turned upside down. She had finally found out the truth, in the worse way Hannah had imagined. Well, not the entire worst. The worst would have been if Dale had laid a hand on *her*. The thought made Hannah suddenly jump up, causing her to grimace in agony. What would he do to her when he found her? Would he keep pretending nothing had happened, or would he silence her into submission? The thought was unbearable, more so than the pain in her side.

Hannah forced herself up onto her knees. She was still struggling to breathe. She knew she was too winded to move very far. There was no way she could beat Dale and Phil to Chrissie on foot. She needed a car.

Hannah crawled on hands and knees back to her bedroom. She had dumped her bag at the foot of her bed. She grabbed it, rummaged through the front pocket and found her phone. Reluctantly, she reached into her own pocket and pulled out the scrunched up note she had sworn never to use. She squinted at the numbers, punched them into her mobile and dialled.

CHAPTER 9

Amanda

Amanda stood absent mindedly stirring the noodles in the pot as she prepared dinner. Danny wasn't home and Tyler and Jenna were outside. She had nearly jumped out of her skin when her phone had buzzed on the bench beside her. She glanced at the unfamiliar number flashing at her from her phone. She didn't normally answer numbers she didn't recognise, yet this was a mobile, so surely not a telemarketer. She dragged the little green telephone symbol across her screen. "Hello?"

"Amanda?" the voice sounded shaky. "Speaking" she replied. "It's Chrithina. Thee's run away, I don't know what to do. I need to find her."

She had only just given her the sticky note, but Hannah was the last person she'd been expecting to call. Her speech was slurred and she was speaking so fast it made it even harder to understand "Hannah? Slow down, what's happened, where are you?"

She let the spoon rest above the pot as she pressed the phone close to her ear and blocked out the sound of the TV with her other hand. "I'm at home. I don'no wad to do. I need a car, I need to find her."

"Ok, ok take a breath Han it will be ok, I'm coming right now."

She waited for a response, but the line dropped, or Hannah had hung up. She put the phone in her pocket and looked at her unfinished dinner, contemplating. She looked at her watch. Danny should be home any minute. Could she rely on Tyler to watch over her dinner? It wasn't exactly responsible of her.

She turned the stove off and made her way outside. "Ty? I need you to look after Jen for a minute. Your dad will be home real soon. There's a boiling pot of noodles on the stove, please don't touch it or let your sister anywhere near it. Tell your father I won't be long, I've er, left something urgent at work. You two just stay here though ok, I promise I won't be long. Be good and if your dad asks, he literally just missed me."

Tyler opened his mouth but if he was about to argue with her he was too late. Amanda shut the door, grabbed her keys and headed out the garage door.

 Amanda hopped into her car and tried to ignore the million scenarios of all the things that could go wrong. Danny would not be impressed, but hopefully he would understand. Besides, it was a good test for Tyler. She laughed to herself, she really could justify anything. Maybe she should have just taken them both along with her, but the way she saw it that was even more irresponsible. She didn't know what she would find, she only knew Hannah had to be desperate for her to call, especially so soon.

Amanda spotted Hannah as she drew closer to the house. She was waiting out the front where her mattress had been. Amanda had barely come to a halt when Hannah rushed over, opened the passenger seat and hopped in.

Amanda couldn't help but notice that Hannah's nose had been bleeding. For one, she carried a blood stained tissue and her nose looked red and sore. She also seemed to be in pain, she was crouched in her seat as though she was experiencing period pain. "What happened?" Amanda asked. "I don' hab time to exblain." Hannah swallowed, took a deep breath and continued. "I think I know where she is. Take a left at the next street, then drive all the way to the end. There's a park on the left. I think she's there. I just hope she's alone." Her speech seemed to be improving. Amanda didn't reply. Instead she followed her instructions. She sensed that this was not the right time for questions.

They pulled up at the park but Hannah didn't move. Amanda waited and looked across at her. She looked scared and confused. She had been so desperate to find her and now they had reached the place she thought she was most likely to be, she didn't want to act. "Hannah? Did you maybe want to go check out the playground? She could be in the cubby or in the shelter above the slide? The rest of the place looks deserted so I think we're ok?"

Hannah remained silent. Amanda opened her door. "I don't know if she'll want to see me," Hannah said suddenly. "You're her sister, she loves you, why wouldn't she want to see you?"

Hannah shrugged and looked out the window. "I'll go if you like?" Hannah nodded. Amanda stepped out of the car and made her way to the cubby house.

She didn't know what to make of Hannah's behaviour, all she knew was she was clearly upset and feared how Chrissie would react to whatever had happened.

"Chrissie?" Amanda called out. She ducked her head under the door of the cubby, but there was no Chrissie. She peered up at the top of the slide, where she thought she could spot a pair of shoes peeking out from the shadows. "Chrissie? It's OK, it's me, Mrs Carson. You can come out, it's alright." Chrissie moved her head from out of the shadows. "Mrs Carson? What are you doing here?"

"I've come to make sure you're alright. Your sister is with me, she asked for my help."

Chrissie peered around but didn't seem convinced. "Where is she?"

"She's waiting in the car, she didn't know if you'd want to see her."

"Is she ok?"

"She's fine, she'll be better once she sees you though." Chrissie peered out of the shelter and looked out towards the car. The sight of the car seemed to reassure her and she crawled out and knelt on top of the slide. She sat for a moment, starring at the car. "If I come down, are you going to take us home?"

"Do you want to go home?" Chrissie didn't respond. She just looked down at her feet.

"It's ok if you don't. I don't have to take you home if you don't want to."

"Does Hannah want to go home?"

"I haven't asked her. She seemed more worried about you. I'm sure she'll go wherever you want to go."

Chrissie whispered and Amanda had to lean in to hear her. "I don't want to go home," she said.

Chrissie slid down the slide and walked with Amanda back to the car. She starred at Hannah through the window with a stunned expression on her face. She opened up the passenger seat behind Hannah and hopped in. The sisters remained silent for the short trip back to the house. Amanda had inspected Chrissie closely but she appeared to be unharmed. What on earth had happened? Hannah seemed completely out of it, she hadn't even lectured Amanda not to ask Chrissie any questions. She just sat there, silently starring out the window.

They pulled into the garage and the girls got out of the car. Amanda waited for communication between them but it never came. "This is my house Chrissie. Why don't you go on inside, I'll introduce you to my daughter." Chrissie nodded and looked at her sister, seeking the go-ahead. "It's ok, I'm right behind you," said Hannah, finally.

They stepped inside and Amanda was relieved to see Tyler and Jenna in front of the TV, unharmed, no smoke, house still intact. Danny wasn't home yet. "I'm back guys. Jen, come here a minute, there's someone I'd like you to meet. Han, why don't you join Ty on the couch and I'll finish dinner?"

Hannah nodded and took the seat furthest from Tyler. "Ah,

you're back," said Tyler. "Did you miss us? Woah, what happened to your face!?"

"I…ran into a door," Hannah replied, lamely.

Amanda peered over at the two of them. Hannah seemed ok and Tyler was harmless anyway, at least he might take her mind off whatever it was that was keeping her so dazed. "Jen, this is Chrissie, Hannah's sister and one of the girls in my class. Chrissie, this is my daughter Jenna. Why don't you girls go upstairs and play, dinner will be ready soon."

The girls obeyed and headed up the stairs towards Jenna's bedroom. Amanda headed back to the kitchen to continue with her dinner. She would have to ask Hannah what had happened, but she wasn't expecting any answers. What would Danny say when he came home and found another girl in the house? Surely he'd understand when she told him they were in trouble. But what proof did she have other than Hannah's nose? She had effectively kidnapped them and now Danny would have to deal with the consequences. She shouldn't have put this on him. She hadn't thought it through, but what choice did she have? Hannah wouldn't have called unless she was desperate.

She childishly thought of hiding them away for the night and escaping his disapproval. This of course was not an option. What a predicament. As if he could sense the pickle of the situation, the garage door sounded to signal Danny's return home. Amanda gulped. '*Here we go,*' she thought.

Danny came through the door and headed straight for the kitchen, bypassing the lounge room and not noticing the extra head above the couch. "This smells amazing honey, I'm starved." He kissed her on the cheek and took a seat at the table. "How was your day?" he asked. She gulped. "It, was er, good. I er, picked up some extra, um…"

"Daddy!" Jenna came racing down the stairs, closely followed by Chrissie. "There's my girl, what have you been up to? You've got a friend with you today, I see?"

"Yes Daddy, this is Chrissie, she's Hannah's sister." Danny pondered this information. Amanda could see his mind ticking over. *Hannah, Hannah… it rings a bell...* and then, lightbulb. He looked at Amanda. "Oh, is she really? And what might Hannah's sister be doing at our house?" He asked Jenna but the question was really directed at Amanda. "Now honey, it's no big deal. I offered for her to stay over because, well you see, her sister is here and well, she's Jen's friend, she can have a friend, can't she?"

"She's Jen's friend? Since when? It's a week night Mandy, I don't think this is a good idea."

Hannah got up off the couch. "It's ok really, we'll just go."

"Hannah no, its fine, sit down."

"Mandy, can I speak with you, privately for a minute?" Amanda sighed and followed Danny to the study. Before he could say anything else, she intervened and explained the situation with as many details as she had.

"So let me get this straight. The girls' parents don't even know where they are? Amanda this is ridiculous, we can't keep them here. You've basically just stolen them off the street. That's what the police will say. I get something bad has happened and you have this need to help people but it's not our problem. We can't just let them stay here, they aren't our responsibility."

"Well they can't go back home, it's not safe. And I didn't *steal* them. Hannah needed me. Their parents more than likely couldn't care less where they are!"

Danny wasn't happy but she wasn't backing down. She would go to their house tomorrow if she had to. "You're putting me in a really bad position you know. Especially at work, if you think these kids are suffering domestic violence, you're supposed to speak up about it. You know that, right?"

"Of course I know that, but they're not saying anything and I don't actually think Chrissie is the one suffering. I think it's Hannah. If we could just find her biological father…"

"And how the hell are we supposed to do that?"

"You know how. There's people at your firm who do this sort of thing for a living, or they know people who do this sort of thing for a living. It just needs a bit of investigating. The sooner we find him the sooner these kids will be out the door."

"You don't know that. Even if we find him, what's to say he even wants anything to do with them? Chrissie isn't even his."

Amanda could feel herself getting emotional. She wasn't even sure why. But if she didn't do something for these kids then who would? And how would she feel when it was too late?

"Please Danny, just think about it. For me?"

She looked at him with her glassy eyes, pleading at him to consider it. He glared at her, knowing he was about to cave. "You know it's practically blackmail when you look at me like that.." He smiled at her. "Fine. I'll think about it. But we can't just keep them here. Their parents have a right to know where they are."

"I honestly don't think they care."

"Well, it's not up to us to decide. I'm not too happy with them being here without their knowledge."

"I know honey, I'll call them tomorrow." And that was that. She had won, for now.

Hannah

Hannah sat on the couch, staring blankly at the TV. Despite it being the comfiest piece of furniture she'd ever had the pleasure of sitting on, she felt anything but comfortable. She was used to feeling unwanted in her own home, but now she was experiencing it at someone else's house. She didn't feel threatened or scared by Danny the way that Dale made her feel, but she still felt the same sense of worthlessness whenever he spoke about her or looked her way. It was obvious that he didn't want the burden of her, and why should he, really? It had been reckless of her to call Amanda. She realised that now. This family didn't need to be bothered with her problems. It was nothing to do with them.

She sat on the couch, eyes pressed on Tyler who was unaware; his eyes were glued exclusively to the television. He didn't realise how easy he had it. He hadn't even flinched when Danny had come home. He hadn't had to set the table, he hadn't had to prepare dinner and he hadn't been smacked across the head for having his feet on the coffee table.

She sighed at him, but he didn't notice. Hannah figured the only thing that would distract him from the screen would be the announcement that dinner was ready. An ad break caused Tyler to temporarily withdraw his attention. He looked across at Hannah and realised she'd been starring at him.

"So, are you gunna tell me what really happened to your nose?" he asked. Hannah looked up towards the kitchen but there was no sign of Amanda or Danny. "I got smacked in the face by a fist," she said simply, yet dramatically. Tyler raised his eyebrows. "By who?"

"My step uncle." Hannah wasn't sure why she was being so honest with Tyler, but part of her was enjoying his reaction. It reflected the seriousness of the situation. "You're bull shitting." Hannah shook her head. "Nope. He's a dead beat. Pretty strong though."

"You're messing with me, aren't you?"

"Maybe I am, maybe I'm not. It's probably best for both of us if you think I *am* messing with you."

Tyler didn't know what to make of this. Was she having him on? Was she trying to impress him? He decided to change the subject. "Did you want to change channel? You can watch whatever you normally watch, I don't care."

"I don't really watch TV." She hadn't said it to sound mysterious and cool. She'd said it because it was the truth. Their TV was probably older than she was. Besides, she didn't want to spend too much time in the open lounge room if she could help it.

"Oh…k then. What do you do when you get home then?"

"I dunno, look after my sister, and try to keep out of trouble."

Again, Tyler wasn't sure if she was serious or not. "What kind of trouble?" he asked. "I mostly try to avoid my step dad, otherwise who knows, I might get another concussion." Tyler chose to ignore what she was implying and instead jumped at the fact that they had something in common. "You've had a concussion? So have I! It's pretty weird huh, waking up in a hospital bed not knowing what's happened?"

"I don't know what that's like. I woke up on my bedroom floor. I don't know why I brought it up really, it's not something I like to think about, let along talk about." She was regretting her carelessness now. Why did she think it was ok to tell Tyler all this? She knew it had been eating her up inside but she hadn't been expecting him to be the person she opened up to. It was stupid, really. She had made things awkward. "How did you get yours?" she asked, trying to take the conversation down a safer path. "Playing footy. I went for a specie and landed on my head. Apparently it looked pretty nasty," he added, proudly. "You should watch me play. It'll give you something to do, keep you out of trouble."

"Right," she replied.

Their conversation was interrupted by Amanda who had returned from her private conversation with Danny. "Hannah, sorry, can I speak with you for a minute?"

Hannah braced herself. '*Here we go,*' she thought.

She followed Amanda into the study where she'd had her meeting with her husband. Hannah had prepped herself for this conversation. "I know he doesn't want us here. I get it. Why would he? I'm sorry I called you. I overreacted."

"Hannah, don't be silly. That's not true. Not entirely. It's not that he doesn't want you here. And he has a name by the way, Danny. Anyway, I want you here and I want to help. But I do have questions about…"

"I'd rather you didn't."

"About your real dad," Amanda finished. "Oh. This again," she said, rolling her eyes once again. "I really think you should try and find him."

"We've been through this. He doesn't want to be found. And like he'd want to meet me anyway. You think it's so easy to just find him? You realise I'm 15 right? He hasn't been around for 15 years. It's pretty much impossible." "Hannah, listen to me. I've told you before, Danny has connections."

"Yeah, great, cool. Even if he did, why would he want to help me?"

"Because *I* want to help you. Maybe things happen for a reason. Maybe you met me as a way of getting closer to finding him. And really, you don't have a choice. You said yourself you can't stay here. But I don't think you should go back home. And you don't know that he wouldn't want to meet you. I don't think he even knows you exist."

"What would you know?" Hannah's temper was rising now. This was pointless advice. Her dad didn't want her. He was just another person who could cause her pain. What if she did find him and he walked away? How would she feel then? Worse than she did now? How could she handle that?

"I know you're upset, but surely it's worth finding out. Even if you don't do it for you. Think of your sister."

"My sister has a dad."

"Oh great, your sister has a dad. So you're happy for me to take her back to him right now? Shall I go get her, then?" Amanda made her way out the door. "No, wait." Amanda stopped. "You don't get it. I don't know anything about him, how the hell am I supposed to find him? I'm just going to get my hopes up about something that's never going to happen. You're telling me I'm just meant to find my dad and it's all one big happy ending? Life isn't like that. Not mine anyway."

Amanda looked at her sympathetically. "No, I'm not saying that. Yes, there is every chance he wants nothing to do with you, of course that's a possibility. But there's also a chance that he'll want to meet you and then, who knows? Honestly Hannah, with the way things are now, can you honestly tell me it's not worth finding out? What have you got to lose?"

For Hannah's entire life she had lived with the prospect of finding her dad. It had given her hope and something to dream of. The idea that she might actually find him scared her. It meant she *did* have something to lose.

"Anyway, dinner should be ready. Just think about it, ok. Any information you might have about him could be really helpful. Take a seat at the table and I'll fetch everyone else."

The 6 of them sat at the table with their stir fry noodles. Jenna was the only one who wasn't touching hers. She was too busy filling in Chrissie on her day at school. Hannah was pleased to see that Chrissie appeared to be ok. She was totally distracted by Jenna, trying to keep up with her every word as she slurped her noodles. Danny avoided Hannah's eye. He instead looked from Amanda, to Jenna, to Tyler. "Oh, Ty I forgot to tell you," he said suddenly as his eyes fell on his son and triggered an earlier conversation. "I spoke with your coach this afternoon. You have to sit out this week I'm afraid mate."

"What? Why?"

"They won't let you play after a concussion. It's mandatory sorry buddy, nothing I can do about it."

"That's bull! I feel completely fine!"

"It doesn't matter how you feel, you can't play."

"Who made that rule up? It's crap."

"Actually, it's not. It's for your safety, it makes perfect sense."

"IT DOES NOT!" Tyler rose his voice. "Plenty of people have concussion and play the next week, why can't I?" "There's no point arguing Ty, it's done."

Tyler slammed his fork on the table and got up out of his seat. He went to leave the room. "Honey, sit down, finish your dinner." Amanda tried to calm him. "No, I'm full," he said and headed out the back door.

'*Why all the fuss over a stupid football match?*' thought Hannah. If she'd carried on like that she'd have copped it big time. Danny made to get up and follow him but Amanda stopped him. "Just leave him be, ok? Give him a minute. He'll be right."

"He's got to get better at dealing with things when they don't go his way."

"I know honey, but you of all people should know how much missing a game will kill him. Especially when he thinks he's fine." Danny sighed.

Hannah peered around after Tyler who had sat himself on the deck outside with his arms crossed. He looked completely shattered.

"Thanks for dinner, I'm full," said Hannah and she picked up her plate and put it in the dishwasher.

She followed Tyler outside and took a seat on the corner of the deck. "Guess you won't be watching me play this week, then," said Tyler as she sat down. "Not this week. But you play the week after right? I can watch you then."

"If I play."

"Why wouldn't you? It sounded like you just have to miss one week?"

"It's bloody stupid."

"It's not really, though. Concussion is obviously pretty serious. I wish someone looked out for me like that."

She said it to herself but it came out out loud. Tyler looked across at her, analysing her. "Things are pretty messed up for you at home, aren't they?" Hannah didn't say anything, she was too scared of what she might tell him. She bit her lip and nodded. "You'll just have to stay here," he said and smiled at her.

"It's not that simple. I think I have to try and find my dad."

"Where is he?"

"No idea. I don't even know his name. He left before I was born."

"Seriously? How are you supposed to find him then!?" Hannah shrugged.

"What will you do if you can't find him?"

"Dunno, go back home I guess."

Hannah tried to make it sound meaningless, like the thought of going home was no big deal. The idea of it though, made her shudder, it gave her goosebumps. She wasn't sure how well she had disguised her fear. The two of them sat in silence for a while. Tyler continued to stare at her, taking it all in.

"Thanks," he said, out of the blue. "For what?" Hannah asked, puzzled. "For putting things in perspective," he said, and headed back inside.

CHAPTER 10

Amanda

Amanda stood apprehensively at the front door. She probably shouldn't be here, yet she knew she would be. She hadn't slept the night before. Instead she had ran over her plan over and over until each moment, up until now, was thought out inside her head. She had blitzed through the morning, getting everyone up and ready with ease. Danny had left before she'd even got out of bed, so she had avoided his lecture – for now. He wasn't going to be happy that she'd stopped at the Uniform shop after dropping off Hannah to buy her and her sister new sets of clothes.

Amanda snapped herself back to the present, glancing at her watch. She still had 20 minutes of her lunch break remaining. She would probably only need 5.

The house was just as gloomy in the daylight as it had been the night she had picked up Hannah in the pouring rain. She took a deep breath and knocked on the door. She thought she could hear movement, but no one came.

She knocked again.

There was definitely someone home and she wasn't leaving until she had confronted them.

"Hello?" she called out. In the middle of her third knock the door was flung open and she was met by a lady that looked a whole lot older than Hannah's mother. Except that she wasn't old. The dark marks under her eyes and the scabs on her face could have initially been mistaken for age, yet Amanda knew they were the effects of years of drug abuse. She wasn't sure that was the only form of abuse either. "Can I help you?" the lady asked tonelessly. Amanda caught her breath and tried to focus as Hannah's mum starred at her impatiently with one hand on her hip. "Um, yes, you see I'm Amanda, I'm Chrissie's teacher and…"

"I don't know where she is."

"Yes I realise that, but it's ok, she's at school.."

"So she's fine? What do you want then?"

Amanda felt her temper rising. Was this woman for real!?

"Well, I just thought you might like to know that Chrissie and Hannah stayed with us last night. That's if you even realised they weren't here."

"What, do you think I'm stupid? Of course I realised."

"Right, you just don't really care."

"Look, I don't know who you think you are coming to my house like this, but you need to leave. For your information, Hannah is a good for nothing and she's always running off. I figured she and her sister were most likely at a friend's house. She does that sometimes."

"I'm sorry, a good for nothing? Have you seen the state of your house? Both your daughters don't want to come home. There's something very wrong about that, isn't there? What kind of mum are you?"

"Damnit woman if you don't get off my property right now, I'm calling the police."

"Good, call them. Perhaps you can explain to them why your daughter is borderline anorexic and has strange bruisings on her body? I sure hope you're not too stupid to realise *that*."

Amanda was shaking now. The woman just stood there, speechless. Amanda wasn't sure but she thought she could see Leanne's eyes glass over.

"Please, just leave. Keep the girls with you for all I care. God knows they'd be better off.." She tapered off and her last sentence was barely a whisper. Amanda almost felt sorry for her.

She seemed so helpless and defeated.

"You don't have to do this you know. Stay I mean. Live like this. We all have choices.."

She'd gone too far. Why did she always go too far?

"Don't you dare." Leanne's nostrils flared, her eyes no longer appeared glassy. "Think you can come here and tell me how to live my life?! You have no idea. You better leave right now, I'm warning you woman."

Amanda began to retreat, but she wasn't quite done. "At least you know now, I've done my bit. You know where your daughters are, they're with Chrissie's teacher, ok? You can find me at the school. Perhaps don't let your boyfriend in on that though, that's my last piece of advice."

She turned and raced to her car. "You can shove your advice right up your.."

Amanda got into her car and slammed the door. She drove around the corner and parked on the side of the road, catching her breath.

Had that gone to plan? She wasn't sure. She had at least let Leanne know her daughters' whereabouts, but now she wasn't sure that was the right move. What if she did tell her boyfriend? Had she put them all in danger? Or was Leanne too far off her rocker to even remember she'd had the conversation?

Amanda put the car back in ignition and made her way back to school. The rest of the day was uneventful and she waited for Hannah with Chrissie after class.

Before long, Hannah showed up around the corner and grabbed Chrissie's bag. *'She always seems so distant,'* thought Amanda. "Hey Hannah, how was your day?" Hannah took a while to respond. She played with Chrissie's hair, twirling it around her finger. "Fine," she said and she edged Chrissie to the footpath to start their walk home. "Actually Hannah, I was thinking. Would the two of you like to stay at mine again tonight?" Hannah

rolled her eyes. "I don't think that's really an option is it?"
"Why not?"
"Hmm let's see. One. Danny. Two. My mum and Dale. Three…"
"Yes Hannah, about that…" Amanda considered the conversation. It was probably best just between the two of them. "Chrissie, I've got an idea for class tomorrow. Would you mind collecting all the dandelions you can find and bring them to me? I need at least 23." Chrissie obeyed and rushed off, pulling out her hat and placing each flower inside it.
"So… I ah, stopped off at your place this afternoon…" Hannah looked up at her and Amanda couldn't tell if she was angry or fearful. "Why would you do that?" she asked.
"Well, they have a right to know where you are, so I was doing the right thing."
 "Right. I'm sure they were real concerned" said Hannah sarcastically. "Well, I only met your mum."
  "She's a real treat, isn't she?" Hannah didn't look at Amanda, she just starred off into the distance. "Actually, she was… I don't know."
"Pathetic? Miserable? Crazy? Delusional? All of the above?" Amanda pondered, "Perhaps all of the above?" She said and thought she caught a wry smile. "Yep. She's an idiot. I bet she didn't even care where we were." "Well, honestly, not really. Or at least she pretended she didn't." Hannah sighed. "She's not pretending. But yeah, sure, believe that if it makes you feel like she's not such a bad person. She doesn't give a toss, although I've got to say I thought she might have at least cared about Chrissie. Normally she does, but heck, she's probably fallen to a new low by now."
 Amanda could sense Hannah's hurt. It was like her mum had betrayed her to the point beyond forgiveness. As far as Amanda could tell, that was fair enough on Hannah's part. It was pretty plain to see she was far from a good parent.
"Has she always been like this?" Amanda wondered out loud.

"Who cares? She's like this now. What's the point thinking about how she used to be? She's a lost cause now."

Amanda could feel the frustration build up inside her. She needed to find this kid's father. She had to give her something. She was completely lost. Hannah spoke so conclusively, like this was just the way things were and there was nothing to be done about it. "I'm sorry you saw her. I'm sorry you wasted your time," said Hannah. "It wasn't a complete waste. She knows where you are, in fact she told me you could both stay, which is what I was actually getting at. You can stay with us." She said it conclusively, attempting to be positive.

"There's still the other problem. Danny." Amanda brushed that off. "I'll talk him 'round," she said simply. "Why are you so hell bent on having us stay? Are you pushing for 'mum of the year' or something? Doing your good deed? There's got to be something in it for you, I just can't work out what it is."

"Wow Hannah, you're on to me. Yep, I'm going for mum of the year, think I have a shot?"

"Well, I've seen worse," Hannah sighed again. Amanda felt like she was getting somewhere, ever so slowly.

Chrissie was making her way back with a hat full of yellow. Hannah turned towards Chrissie, but her eyes had glazed over and she had the look as though she were a million miles away. Amanda wondered where exactly her mind wondered. "She was pretty once, you know." Hannah said suddenly. "Sorry, what?"

"My mum. She used to be pretty. Can you believe that?" Amanda didn't know what to say. "Who cares now though, right? Like I said, who cares about the way things were."

Amanda didn't say anything, all she could feel was a complete sense of helplessness. Her awkward silence was saved as Chrissie came bounding up to them, showing off her collection. "Look Ms! I think I got every single one in the grounds! There must be 100!"

"Your next job is to count them all" said Hannah who had turned into a different person at the sight of Chrissie's excitement. "Oh Han, you must be joking!"

"I sure am" she said with a laugh and she made her way to the staff carpark. "Are we not going home?" Asked Chrissie. "I think we'll stay with Ms Carson again, if that's ok with you?" Chrissie couldn't contain her excitement. "Wait 'til I show Jenna!"

Amanda smiled at them both. She had to hand it to Hannah. She could be so flat, like she had the weight of the world on her shoulders, yet she could switch it all off for the sake of her sister. Amanda couldn't help think about the way things must have been, or no doubt could have been, if Leanne hadn't fallen for Dale. Like Hannah said, there was no point dwelling in the past, but Amanda knew Hannah still thought about it too. Amanda couldn't put her finger on exactly why she was so desperate to help, all she knew was that Hannah deserved so much more, and if Amanda could help her find it, then the real question was, why not?

Jenna was ecstatic to find Chrissie in the car as Amanda picked her and her brother up. Amanda couldn't help but notice Tyler seemed equally as excited to see Hannah who had left the front seat vacant for Tyler. "So, I take it you're staying with us again then?" he asked, turning around in his seat to talk to her. "Looks like it," replied Hannah. "Cool." He opened his mouth to continue the conversation, but Hannah was staring blankly out the window, appearing in no mood for conversation. A little put out, he drew his attention instead to his mum. "So… I'm sorry I cracked it last night mum. I get why I can't play on the weekend."

"Oh, so you've come round just like that huh? You're sounding very different to last night."

"Yeah well, I guess you can thank Hannah for that. Did you know she's had a concussion too?"

He said it before he could stop himself. Hannah snapped out of her daydream and shoved the back of his seat. He looked back at her apologetically. "Yeah, but anyway, it's no big deal." He was digging a hole for himself now. "Right. No one else's injuries could possibly be a big deal compared to yours, when you have to miss out on an entire football match for one whole week. Right, Hannah?" Hannah could tell Amanda was trying to engage Hannah, attempting to sense if she should be concerned about this new information, but she didn't reply. She was too angry to say anything. What was he doing bringing up something so personal? Why did she bother opening up her mouth to anybody? She continued to stare out the window. Tyler remained silent for the remainder of the trip.

As they got out of the car Tyler approached Hannah. "I'm sorry, I don't know why I said that, it just slipped out."

 "Forget about it. Like you said, it's no big deal." She moved passed him and followed Amanda inside. Tyler felt bad but he didn't know what else to do. Was it really that bad? She hadn't said how she had got concussion. He didn't even know how she had, other than what she had been implying. Maybe that was the point. It had been a discussion between the two of them. He wasn't even entirely sure she'd meant to have it with him. It was like it had slipped out when she'd said it too, like it was a secret.

Hannah

"So, are you going to try and find your dad?" Tyler asked as they again sat in front of the TV. "I don't know."

Hannah couldn't be bothered with Tyler or his questions. She didn't feel like talking. Tyler wasn't going to give up that easily though. "Well, I think you should." "Right."

"'Cause I mean, you can't just stay here forever, and you can't go back home. So you should try and find him."

"Right," she said again. "But where are you going to start. Do you know where he lives?" She just looked at him, rolling her eyes. "I take that as a 'no'. How are you going to find him then?"

"I don't know Tyler, honestly can you give it a rest?" "Sorry, I'm just curious. I mean, it will be hard when you don't even know what he looks like, right?"

"Right."

Chrissie looked up suddenly. "But you do know what he looks like!"

"No, I don't." She was being short with Chrissie now too. "Yes, you do."

"Well, yeah ok, so I know he has the same eye colour and hair colour as me, that's not really that helpful. Plenty of people have brown hair and blue eyes." She was tired of being pestered with questions, and now her sister was joining in with stupid comments. Chrissie looked at her, confused. "But Han, you've seen the photo, you know what he *looks* like." It was Hannah's turn to be confused. "What photo?"

"Mum's photo. In her photo album. Honestly Han, how can you not remember?"

"What do you mean? What photo album? What photo"

Hannah was interested now, but it was Chrissie's turn to roll her eyes. She huffed and continued her story. "You know the photo. The one mum gets out every time she's acting all funny when daddy's not around." Hannah stared at her blankly. "Honestly Chrissie I do not know what you're talking about. Mum's never shown me any photo?"

"But she must have. She always gets out the same photo. She's shown me at least 3 times. She gets it out and tells me stories."

"She tells you stories about my real dad?"

"Mmhm."

"What does she say?"

"I don't know, all kinds of things."

"Let me get this straight. You know all about my real dad, and you've never said anything?"

"You're the one who never talks about him. You get all weird whenever I've asked about him."

It was true that Hannah didn't particularly like speaking about him. She never liked speaking about him to Chrissie because well, he wasn't *her* dad and she thought it would make her feel uncomfortable. But she had no idea Chrissie knew more about him than she did. She was always under the impression that her mum knew nothing about her dad. She was never keen to talk about him, not to her anyway. As far as Hannah was aware they had had a fling, a one night stand, he had meant nothing. Hell, she described him as a 'deadbeat', what on earth was she doing with a photo of him!?

"I can't believe mum has told you all this stuff, she's shown you a bloody picture and I know nothing!" Chrissie shrugged her shoulders.

"Sorry, I thought you knew. I didn't know you wanted to find him."

Hannah had to catch her breath, let it all sink in. All this time, Leanne had been confiding her feelings to Chrissie whenever she was drunk. All this time, she had a means of finding him, a clue at least, but Leanne had never let on, never shown her the picture, and never told her anything. No, she had expressed her feelings to her precious 5 year old daughter, her wanted daughter.

Hannah felt hurt and betrayed, which was nothing new, really. "I'm sorry Hannah," Chrissie said softly. "It's ok kiddo. It's not your fault." Hannah put her arm around her. "Do you know where mum keeps the photo album?"

"Yeah, it's under her bed." Hannah contemplated this. She needed to get her hands on it. Chrissie looked at her curiously. "You're not going to go back there, are you?" she asked fearfully.

Hannah looked at her sympathetically. The kid was clearly tormented by what she had seen and was petrified at the thought of going back home. '*Welcome to my world*,' Hannah thought.

"Maybe, I'm not sure. But whatever I decide, you can stay here."

Chrissie didn't say anything. She just sat there, too frightened to speak.

"Anyway, it's not for you to worry about, kiddo. Why don't you go find Jenna, I'm sure she'd like someone to play with?" Chrissie looked as though she didn't want to move, but she obeyed her sister and headed upstairs to find Jenna.

"You're going to go back, aren't you?" Tyler prompted. Hannah shrugged her shoulders. "Seriously, I don't know if you should. I mean, I didn't really believe you at first, but now your sister is acting all strange and I really don't think you should go back." Hannah could hear the concern in Tyler's voice and it somehow helped calm her. It was like a confirmation that she wasn't just dramatizing the whole thing, it was affirmation that what she put up with definitely wasn't normal. Of course, she knew this already, but it was nice to have someone else acknowledge it too.

"I have to go back." She said. "I have to find him. That photo is the perfect place to start. It's the only place." Tyler looked defeated. "I'm coming with you, then," he said suddenly. "Are you out of your mind!?"

"Well, your mind is clearly made up and I know I'm not going to stop you, so I'll come with you." He said it matter-of-factly, like that was the end of the discussion.

"I don't think so."

"You can't stop me."

"Actually, I can. You don't even know where I live for a start. I'll just go there during school."

"I know where your school is. I'll just hang out and wait for you."

"And wag class?" She raised her eyebrows. What would dear mummy and daddy say if their private-school son skipped class? She sniggered. "So what? You're going to need a hand. Besides, mum's trying to help you anyway, I don't think she'll care if I wag class if it means I'm helping you."

"Why don't you tell her your expert plan then?"

"Maybe I will." Hannah sniggered again, ending the conversation.

It got her thinking, though. She needed a plan. Was it really such a good idea to go during school hours? Dale had said he would be home all week.

Yet she couldn't go after school. He was more likely to have started drinking, his friends usually headed over in the evening and dealing with Dale alone was a big enough problem. But the album was under the bed, right where he slept. She couldn't exactly risk sneaking in at night and hope he was too stoned to wake.

Maybe she did need Tyler. He could lend a hand, maybe work as a distraction. She was unsure though. Amanda might not mind if he skipped class for her sake, but Danny definitely would. He wouldn't like Tyler helping her at all, at any time. She didn't really want to cause trouble. As much as she disliked Danny, he had let her stay, even when he hadn't wanted her to. Still, she would feel better if she had someone with her. When it came down to it, it was Tyler's decision if he wanted to come or not. He was right, she couldn't stop him.

Amanda announced that dinner was ready, distracting Hannah from her thoughts. Jenna bounced down the stairs with Chrissie following slowly behind. She still didn't look herself.

As they sat down to eat, Chrissie sat glumly, not touching her dinner. She got up off her seat and placed her plate in the sink. She didn't say anything or look at anyone, instead she made her way silently onto the couch. Hannah took one last bite and followed her.

"What's up, kiddo? I didn't mean to scare you before." Chrissie didn't look at her sister. She just stared down at her hands. "Look, I'm not going to lie to you. I probably will go back. But I'll be careful, maybe Tyler will come with me, we'll be safe.."

"It's not that, it's just…"

"What is it?"

"What if you find your dad? Where will I go?" Chrissie had tears in her eyes. Hannah hadn't been expecting that. She hadn't even thought far enough ahead to wonder what would happen if she actually did find her dad. Clearly her sister was one step ahead.

"Hey, it's ok, we'll sort it out. I'm not even going to find him. It's just a photo." But what *would* happen to Chrissie if she found her dad? She wasn't sure, but she couldn't really think about it. After all, was it even worth worrying about? The chances of finding him were extremely slim anyway. Even if she did, he probably wouldn't even want to meet her.

She didn't know how to comfort her sister. She hadn't exactly planned on giving her something else to worry about.

Before she could comfort her, Jenna stepped in and begged Chrissie to go back to her bedroom to play.

As the two of them headed back upstairs, Tyler took Chrissie's place on the couch.

"So what's our plan of attack?" Tyler whispered.

"I don't know, I just know I've got to get my hands on that photo."

"Yeah, but how exactly? What will happen if your mum finds you there?"

"It's not my mum I'm worried about."

"Right. Well what will happen if your dad, I mean, step dad, finds you there?"

"Look, it's a risk I'm not exactly willing to take. But I don't have a choice. Without that photo, I have no leads."

"You really are keen to find him then, huh?"

"I guess so. I have to know who he is. If I don't, I'm just going to think about it my whole life. I've done that enough already."

"So are you really going to go during the day? Wouldn't it be better to sneak in at night when they're asleep?" "Given that the photo is in their bedroom, where they'll both be sleeping, I don't think that's the smartest idea." "So what, you think going in broad daylight is a better idea?"

"Yeah, I guess so. They might not even be home then. I can just sneak in and grab the photo, they won't even know."

"Can you be sure they won't be home?"

"No, but like I said, I still think it's the best option."

"It sounds risky."

"Yeah, sorry, it's probably too much for your poor concussed brain to handle." Tyler looked offended. "You know I'm going to come with you."

"Ha ha, and what help will you be? I'll be fine on my own," she teased. Tyler ignored her, he just continued as if she hadn't said anything. "Seriously though, what will you do if they *are* home?"

"I'll have to come back another time." Tyler raised his eyebrows.

"I can't see that happening. You'll want to get it, right then and there."

"So maybe I will. Honestly Tyler, if you don't want to come, I honestly don't care."

"No, I do want to, I want to help you."

"I've noticed. What is up with you and your mum and 'helping' people?"

"So? Shouldn't you be happy we want to help? You know, if we told mum the plan, she *would* help."

"Ok, you're not actually serious about telling your mum about this?"

"Why not? She's got a car, it'd be a quick getaway."

"I really didn't pick you for a mummy's boy."

"And I didn't pick you for an idiot. Stubborn, yes. An idiot, no. Guess I was wrong."

Hannah rolled her eyes. "If you think you're going to change my mind by calling me names, you've really got me totally wrong."

"Why have you got a thing against letting people help you?"

Hannah sighed. "So say you come with me. You have to be ready to do as I say. For one, you'd have to meet me at my school – do you even know how to get there?"

"I'd figure it out."

"I don't have time for you to 'figure it out.' I'm going to go tomorrow. If you haven't figured it out by then that's not my problem. If you're not outside the gate at 1 o'clock, I'm going without you."

"I still think you should tell my mum."

"I either go with you, or I go on my own, that's the deal." "Fine. I'll see you at 1 then."

"Fine." And that was that.

CHAPTER 11

Hannah

Hannah was dropped off at school, but she didn't even go. She couldn't be bothered speaking to Tess and she didn't really want to tell her why she was skipping class at 1 o'clock, or why she didn't want her to come with her. She couldn't even really explain to herself why she didn't want to tell her best friend what had happened. There was just something inside her that couldn't fully trust her. It wasn't exactly a new feeling. Hannah didn't really trust anybody. Yet she had told Tyler, some guy she had known all of 5 minutes, a lot more than she should have. And then there was his mother. Hannah sighed to herself. What was she thinking? She glanced at her watch. 12.58pm. *'You've got two more minutes and I'm out of here, Tyler,'* she thought to herself.

She leant against the fence and heard the sound of a car approaching slowly. She turned her head and saw the very same four wheel drive that had pulled up in the rain. The same car that she had hopped in and out of to and from school for the past few days. *'I am going to kill Tyler,'* she thought to herself as Amanda wound down the window.

Amanda

When Amanda had heard the news of the photograph, it had come as a shock. A happy, exciting, thrilling shock. It provided an opportunity, a glimmer of hope. Now, just maybe, the photo could lead them to Hannah's biological father. Of course, it was farfetched. After all, the photo had to be at least 15 years old, and what were the chances of it actually leading to an identity? She hadn't even seen the photo. It could be out of focus, it could be completely useless. Still, it didn't stop her from feeling a sense of hope and wonder. She had been proud of Tyler for coming to her too. It showed maturity, trust and above anything else, responsibility. Hannah wouldn't think so of course. But with her help maybe she would change her mind. She laughed to herself as she imagined Hannah's face when she showed up. Independent, secretive, suspicious Hannah would hate that she was getting involved – again. She would just have to learn that the two of them were in this together, whether she liked it or not.

Amanda couldn't remember the last time she had called in sick. Had there even been a last time? She knew she had definitely never lied about being sick. At least, not until this morning. She had thought about her plan over and over in her head, and there simply was no other alternative. It was the only option. Her lunch break didn't exactly fall at the right time to help Hannah, and even if it did there could be no certainty of exactly how long Hannah would be.

And so, she had decided – she would call in sick and avoid all complications. No one knew her plan except Tyler which in itself was strange. Amanda sensed that Tyler wasn't impressed with himself for confiding in his mum, no doubt he felt guilty that he wasn't the one saving the day himself. She had reassured him that everything would be fine before she grabbed her phone to make the call. She hadn't actually managed to get a hold of Jenny and she felt slightly guilty about leaving a voice mail message explaining why she was too sick to come in. She hadn't heard back from her so she assumed it was all ok.

As Amanda pulled up to the gates outside Hannah's school, she spotted the teenager who as predicted, was not happy to see her.

"What do you think you're doing here?" she asked disapprovingly.

"I'm here to help, of course."

"I should have known Tyler wouldn't be able to keep his mouth shut. Had to run to mummy, didn't he?"

"Yes, you can thank him later," said Amanda coolly.

"Ha! Unlikely."

"So, are you going to keep sulking or are you going to get in the car?"

Hannah raised her eyebrows at Amanda's new approach. Amanda was over playing nice. Besides, didn't Hannah realise by now that she was here to help her?

"I don't really have a choice, do I?"

"Glad you've caught on. Hop in."

"So, what's the plan?" asked Amanda as Hannah did up her seatbelt. Hannah glared at her, but sensing it was a loss cause to argue, she responded.

"Well, first I need to suss out if anyone is home. They normally leave the back door open. If the coast is clear I'll go through there and head straight to the bedroom. Piece of cake."

"And if they *are* home?"

"I don't know. Maybe you can distract them, make yourself useful." She said it with cheek and it made Amanda smile. "I'll see what I can do," she said.

As Amanda approached the house, she pulled the car up on the other side of the road.

"So, how do we do this?" Hannah followed Amanda's eyes and looked across at her house. "Once I figure out if anyone is home I'll come and report back to you. Then, we figure out a plan."

 "Sounds good. Just be careful." Hannah nodded and undid her seatbelt. She got out of the car and crept around to the side of the house. She peered through the window and waited several minutes before she ran across the yard to the front door. She rang the doorbell and ducked behind the bushes. No one came to the door. Still not satisfied, Amanda watched as Hannah disappeared towards the back gate.

After several minutes Hannah returned. "They're not home, and the back door is unlocked. I'm going to go through there and grab the album. You can keep a look out. If you see anything, beep the horn twice and I'll leave."

"Yes ma'am. I'm on the lookout." Hannah gave her a small smile. "Thanks," she said and headed back towards the house.

Hannah

As much as Hannah hated the thought of being back home, the idea of finding a photo of her dad pumped her with adrenalin and she climbed over the back gate fence with her heart racing. Plus, maybe having Amanda to help wasn't such a bad thing. A car could potentially be useful. She opened the laundry door and made her way down the hall to her mum's bedroom. The curtains were closed and the room was dim, but she didn't want to turn on the light in case they returned. The bedroom was visible to the street.

She headed to her mum's side of the bed, knelt down and felt around for an album-shaped object. It didn't take her long to find. It was practically the only thing under there besides a pair of slippers and an old tissue.

She grabbed the album and rose to her feet. Before she could do anything else, the sound of a car horn beeping not once but twice caused her to gasp as the fear crept inside her. What were the chances of them coming back now!?

She could hear the sound of keys and the front door opening. She quickly weighed up her options, knowing that she was too far from the laundry door to escape. She only had seconds. Hannah shoved the album back under the bed and lied down, sizing up the gap between frame and floor. Her small figure enabled her to squeeze herself under and she slid in, just as she heard footsteps approaching the bedroom door. She could see a pair of feet at the doorway that unmistakeably belonged to her mother. She held her breath as her mother approached the bed. Surely she wouldn't know Hannah was there. The sound of the doorbell made Hannah jump and she nearly bumped her head on the bedframe.

Leanne appeared to ignore the sound and she sat down on the bed, her legs resting in front of Hannah's face. The doorbell sounded for a second time and Leanne sighed. "For God's sake," she said and hopped off the bed to answer the door.

Realising her opportunity, Hannah slid out from under the bed, grabbed the photo album and charged for the back door.

As she reached the door she flung it open, ready to race to the fence. Before she could make a move, the sight of an object in motion out the corner of her eye caused her whole body to freeze.

It was like her body had sensed him before her eyes had even registered what they were seeing. Dale was in the backyard, rummaging through the garbage bin with his back turned. Hannah couldn't breathe. If he turned his head he would spot her and she would be trapped. Her mind raced as she entered 'fight or flight' mode. She knew her only option was to jump the fence. She had been stupid to think her mum would have come home by herself. Leanne never went anywhere on her own these days, not unless she was doing her weekly shop, but that was never normally on a Friday.

Thankfully the laundry door had stayed open, meaning Dale hadn't heard Hannah as she stood in the doorway. He seemed eager to find whatever he was looking for, and in doing so seemed temporarily unaware of his surroundings. Hannah knew he couldn't look there forever and she silently ducked down beneath the bushes to wait. She immersed herself in them, camouflaging herself from view.

 She prayed she had hidden herself completely. She was well and truly trapped now if he found her on his way back to the house.

"So that wasn't you at the door? Some idiot rang the bell and ran off."

Hannah bit her lip as her mum stood at the laundry door, oblivious to her daughter kneeling only feet away. "I thought I'd locked you out. What on earth are you doing?" she asked suddenly, realising Dale was practically inside the bin. "I'm looking for something," he replied, frustrated. "Well yes, I can see that. But what?" "Nothing."

"Sure doesn't look like nothing. Tell me what it is and I can help you find it."

"Just fuck off would you."

"Jesus, calm the farm I was only trying to help. Bloody lunatic." She mumbled the last bit under her breath, but Dale wasn't having it. "What did you say?"

"Nothing," she said it in exactly the same tone as he had moments earlier, in much the same way as Hannah would have done. Hannah could sense though that in much the same way, she shouldn't have said it.

Leanne sensed the danger and she headed back inside. She had fired him up though and he stomped back inside after her.

Hannah felt the fear creep back inside her. She hated her mum for so many reasons, including the fact that she was the one who had brought Dale on them all in the first place. Still, she couldn't help but worry about her and what Dale was no doubt about to do. But Hannah was in her own predicament and she needed to leave, fast.

She crept out from her hiding place, tucked the album under her arm and ran to the fence without looking back. She managed to hurl herself over it, dropping the album down onto the ground on the other side. She jumped down off the fence and scooped the album back into her hands. She could hear the yells as she ran to the safety of Amanda's car. Dale was too angry at Leanne to notice Hannah race across the front yard and into the passenger seat of the Range Rover.

Amanda didn't waste any time. She already had the engine going and she got the car in motion before Hannah had even shut the door. Her tyres screeched as she made a sharp turn to exit the street.

Both out of breath, Amanda picked a random road and pulled over. They took a moment to compose themselves as Hannah looked behind her, unable to stop the concern she now felt for her mum. "Are you ok?" Amanda asked. Hannah gulped. "I'm fine. I don't think my mum is though."

She was annoyed with herself for caring, particularly when the same person didn't give one thought about her. "Should we go back?" Amanda asked. Hannah looked at her and felt a sense of appreciation. This strange woman really did care about people. Hannah knew Amanda didn't really want to go back, but she knew she would do it simply for the sake of doing the right thing. And for some bizarre reason, maybe if it was only because Hannah wanted her to.

"No, I can't. I can't go back. I just can't." They sat quiet for a while before Amanda broke the silence. "Hannah, are you ever going to tell me exactly what happens inside that house?"

"Like you can't put two and two together," Hannah replied, glumly. Amanda nodded. "I'm not an idiot. But I mean, you talking about it. I think you need to talk about it." Hannah blinked back the tears that were beginning to build behind her eyes. "What's the point? Besides, we should be talking about *this*," she held up the album and Amanda smiled. "I take it that was you ringing the doorbell, by the way?"

"Yes, it was. And I'm so sorry Hannah, I'm the worst watchdog ever. I got a text message and I was all distracted. I didn't even see them until they were practically at the door."

"Are you kidding, you saved my life! And now I've finally got my hands on this."

Hannah felt a new sense of gratitude towards Amanda. She was the reason she now had her hands on a photo of her dad. Hannah stared down at the album on her lap as a wave of emotions swept over her. She didn't know how to prepare herself for what was inside. For the first time in her life, she was going to see her dad. She would know what he looked like. He wouldn't just be some made up figment of her imagination. From this moment, she would have an actual real picture inside her head every time she thought about him. "So are you going to open it or what?" Amanda asked, the anticipation clear in her voice. "I'm sorry, this is probably something you want to do alone," she added regretfully, as if her enthusiasm had got the better of her. "No, it's ok. It's just, this is it."

Hannah could feel her body tingling. "I know," said Amanda and she made a sudden movement as if she was going to hug her, but seemingly changing her mind, she leant back in her seat.

Hannah propped the album up and decided to start from back to front. She laid the album down so that it opened up onto the last page. Her emotional rollercoaster hit her hard and she was completely overwhelmed as she peered down at the faces in her lap. The tears welled up and escaped from her eyes as she glanced from photo to photo. Nothing could have prepared her as she took each image in. Her younger self smiled back at her, joyful and unknowing. She must have been around the same age as Chrissie was now. She flicked to the next page, unable to control the steady flow of tears as they dropped onto the pages beneath her. There was her mother, 10 years younger, holding Hannah in her arms. '*She almost looks happy,*' thought Hannah sadly as she looked back and pondered what could have been.

She flicked quickly through the pages now, eager to find him. And then, there he was. There was no mistaking him. He had the very same grey-blue eyes as Hannah's, the same mousey hair, maybe even the same smile. He was practically her male version, and only a few years older.

She almost didn't recognise the girl standing beside him, arm in arm. But then, there was something in those eyes Hannah had seen before. She knew her mum had been attractive, she vaguely remembered her in a similar sense to the woman she had seen holding her 5 year old self. She had never known her mum like this though. She was stunning. Her eyes were bright and cheerful, her face was full and beautiful. She seemed so vibrant, so content. But then, there was more than one photo. There were dozens of them. She looked at her dad from all different angles. Pictures on the beach, pictures in the park. Close up photographs of the two of them hand in hand, smiling and laughing. As she looked at each photo it became more and clear. Her dad hadn't been some one night stand. He had been the love of his mum's life, and she had been his. Yet Leanne spoke of him like he was nothing, like he didn't exist. *'What the hell happened?'* thought Hannah as she stared at them both. She tried to form a timeline in her head. They were obviously taken before she was born, but how much earlier?

"Wow, is that your mum?" Hannah jumped. She had been so absorbed she had forgotten Amanda was even there. "Yep, that's her."

"And that's your dad. You look just like him." Amanda peered across at the photos and Hannah handed her the album. "Here." "My gosh, *Hannah*," she said and Hannah looked up at her. Was she crying too?

Amanda

They had just pulled up outside Hannah's house and Amanda sat watching as Hannah jumped out of the car, heading back towards the house. Just as she jumped the fence, she felt her phone vibrate. She reached into her jacket pocket and pulled out her phone. It was Jenny. Panic swept over her. What would she say!? She was meant to be at home. 'Think Amanda, think.' Could she fake a cough? A sneeze perhaps? Before Amanda could decide what to say or do, the call ended. *'Crap,'* she thought. That wouldn't look good. But she could have been sleeping, right? She contemplated returning the call, but she really didn't know what to say. Her phone beeped again, notifying her of a text message. "Hi Mandy, just checking in. Please call me back when you can, I'd like to have a chat. Jen." Amanda gulped. It didn't exactly sound good. Did she know she wasn't really sick? Did she know she had taken the day off to assist her student's sister? Was there anything wrong with helping her student's sister? Amanda's mind raced. How would she explain her way out of this one?

Movement in her peripheral vision caused an all new kind of panic. Leanne and Dale had arrived home. Amanda hadn't even spotted their car pull up. She'd been too busy freaking out about Jenny. 'Shit!' She honked the horn twice as loudly as she could, but Hannah's mum was already stepping inside.

Amanda's mind was racing. She didn't know if Hannah would have enough time to escape without either of them noticing. She had only one choice. Amanda undid her seat belt and hopped out of the car. She ran to the front door and rang the doorbell. She stepped aside so that she wouldn't be seen when they came to the door. Except that no one was coming. '*Come on!*' she thought. She rang the doorbell for a second time and again hid herself from view. This time, it had done the trick. She heard footsteps and the sound of the door opening. It was Leanne. "Hello? Dale, was that you?"

When there was no reply, Leanne closed the door and stepped back inside. Amanda ran back to the safety of her car. "Come on Hannah," she said out loud as she sat back down.

*

Once Amanda had pulled into a side street and they had both caught their breath, she watched as Hannah glanced from photo to photo. It was crazy to think she now had her hands on a photo of her dad. Amanda couldn't help but wonder if it meant she was now a step closer to finding him. Would the photo be enough for Danny and his colleagues to work with? She still wasn't entirely sure he would offer any assistance. Surely he would.

Amanda hadn't even recognised Leanne. The transformation was completely shocking. It disturbed her and it upset her. How could this have happened? How had she *let* this happen?

Amanda contemplated the life Hannah had been brought up with. It was beyond anything she could even comprehend. She gazed at the clock on her dial when suddenly the time dawned on her. "Crap! Hannah, I'm sorry but I should get you back to school. You're going to miss your next class." Hannah looked at her. "Oh, ok," she said, a little upset.

Amanda felt guilty but she also had responsibility. She had done her bit, she couldn't exactly let a student wag class. "I know so much has happened and it's probably the last thing you feel like doing. But I really do need to get you back. We'll talk about this later though ok, I'm sorry."

"Sure, no worries. Thanks. For everything," she gave Amanda a weak smile and packed the album inside her backpack.

Amanda watched Hannah walk back inside the gate towards class until she was out of view. She decided it was best to call back Jenny. She sighed as the line began to ring.

"Hi Mandy, thanks for calling me back, how are you feeling?"

"I'm ok, I've just got a nasty head cold," she tried to make her voice sound tired.

"That's no good. Look, I don't know if this would be better off waiting until next week when you're feeling better, I just wanted to make sure everything was ok?"

"Yeah, I'm fine thanks. I'll be back on Monday. Was there something you wanted to talk about?"

"That's good – it's just – I've noticed you've been taking one of your students' home the past few days. Christina. I just thought – I don't mean to be a sticky nose, but well, it is kind of my job to be."

"Oh, that. No, everything is fine. She's a good friend of Jenna's – my daughter. It's been nice for Jenna to have someone outside her school to play with. She's been – having a bit of trouble. Chrissie has been a big help." She didn't know why she had blatantly lied, but there it was.

"I see. It's just – I don't know if you've noticed but her parents are a bit – how do I put this? They haven't been the most – approachable people. I wasn't sure if you were just dropping her home or if she was staying at yours? I just wanted to check and make sure everything was ok at home – that you haven't noticed anything out of the ordinary?"

Amanda was silent. What was she supposed to say to that? She knew Hannah didn't want anyone nosing in on her life. It had been hard enough gaining her trust – she wasn't even entirely sure she had it, so should she betray it?

"Mandy – are you still there?"

"Sorry, yeah. No, everything is fine as far as I can tell. I mean, I've only met Leanne, Chrissie's mum. She's not exactly the warmest person on earth but she's been fine with me having Chrissie stay over."

She didn't mention that her sister was also staying. There were a lot of things she hadn't mentioned. Had she just dug herself a mighty big hole?

"Ok, I see. Well, if you do notice anything out of the ordinary, please come and see me. Now I'll leave you be, rest up there Mandy, hopefully we'll see you back on Monday."

She hung up, leaving Amanda feeling extremely guilty.

Hannah

Hannah was in a strange mood. She was ecstatic to find photos of her biological father. The photos gave her butterflies. Yet she felt a strange sense of sadness at the same time. They had both looked so happy. She couldn't help but feel like she was the reason everything had fallen apart. She was confused as her emotions went up and down in waves. She needed time to process the last half an hour. Hannah's thoughts were interrupted as

Tess bounded up to her from the locker bay. '*Great,*' she thought. The last thing she felt like doing was sharing her feelings with Tess.

"Yo, Han, where have you been!?" Tess asked, racing up to Hannah. Noticing the large car by the gate, Tess raised her eyebrows. "Who's that?" she asked curiously. "No one," said Hannah tonelessly. "Come on, I just saw you get out of their car. Since when are you friends with rich bitches – or bastards?"

"She's not my friend," Hannah said simply. "Right. So you've just been on a lunch trip with a random? Come on Han, spill the beans. Who is it? You said 'she.' Is it your *girlfriend*? I won't judge I swear. I just want to know. I mean, since when have you been friends with an uptown snob, that's all?"

"I *said*, she's not my friend. And she's definitely not my girlfriend. Just drop it ok?"

Hannah wasn't entirely sure why she was being so distant and cold. She just knew she didn't want to share with Tess that she'd been staying with her sister's school teacher. It implied all new kinds of 'lame' and she simply couldn't be bothered with it. She had enough on her plate already.

"What is up with you lately? I feel like I've done something to upset you."

"Well, your brother hasn't helped," Hannah knew she was using him as an excuse. That wasn't really what was bothering her. She just didn't want to be around Tess right now, she wanted to be alone to deal with her thoughts. "I'm sorry about that, but I'm not my brother. Take your issues with him out on him, not me."

Hannah remained silent. She just couldn't be bothered. She had way too many things on her mind to contemplate. Like her dad and the world he'd left behind. The thought upset her. Why had he left? He had looked so happy. They both did. What had gone so wrong? *Was* she the reason he'd gone?

When Hannah said nothing, Tess continued to probe. "So, are you seriously not going to tell me who that fancy car belonged to?"

"Just forget it, Tess. Seriously," Hannah was getting angry now. She just wanted to be left alone, was that so hard? "Fine, geez! I'll see you later when you don't have PMS!" Tess stormed off, leaving Hannah feeling completely irritated.

She was totally confused by her feelings. She didn't really know why she didn't share her album with Tess and talk to her about everything that had happened. But her feelings were private, she didn't know how to deal with them herself – she didn't want to have to worry about how Tess would deal with them too. Besides, if Tess knew she was staying with a rich family, she would probably try and take advantage. She was that kind of person. Most people were. She didn't want to give Amanda any trouble. As much as she'd hated her for getting involved, she'd helped her and she didn't want to take that for granted.

* *

Hannah, Tyler, Jenna, and Chrissie had been picked up from school. Hannah's mind continued to race as they all sat in front of the TV. She was cold and distracted by the album as the photos she'd seen flashed inside her head. She hadn't mentioned the album again, in fact she'd hardly said a word since Amanda had picked her up. Amanda hadn't probed her either and Hannah was grateful for that. Tyler was strangely silent too. He sat with his eyes fixated on the TV, yet Hannah sensed his mind was also somewhere else. On the other hand, Jenna and Chrissie were glued to the television, 100% devoted to the program in front of them.

Just as Amanda was about to speak, Hannah stood up. "I'm feeling a bit cold. Tyler, would you mind if I borrowed your trackies again?"

"Huh? Ah, yeah sure. They're just upstairs – on my bed I think." Hannah made for the stairs when Amanda stopped her. "Tyler, don't be lazy, go get them for her." "No, it's ok I can get them myself. Tyler's clearly busy watching his favourite show," she smirked and headed upstairs. It was a good excuse to leave the room and avoid conversation. She wondered what Tyler was really thinking about. If she wasn't so entrenched in her own thoughts she would have been curious to find out.

As Hannah reached the top of the stairs she made her way to Tyler's bedroom. He had been right, his track pants were folded neatly on the corner of his bed. As she reached to grab them she stepped on something squishy beneath her feet. She looked down and realised she'd stepped on Tyler's school pants, right above the left pocket. She expected it was a plastic wrapper from a packet of chips or chocolate, but she couldn't help herself. She grabbed the pants and pulled out the unknown object. What she found bewildered her and she was overcome with a deep sense of shock and rage.

She threw the package onto the floor in disgust as she felt her heart race.

"How long does it take to put on a pair of pants?" Tyler asked as he appeared at the doorway, oblivious to Hannah's discovery.

"What the actual fuck?" said Hannah, unable to keep her voice down.

Tyler stood back in shock and then noticed his stash of ice on the floor. He was speechless. For one thing, he couldn't believe he had forgotten about it and had left it carelessly in his school pants. "Seriously, are you fucking insane!? Why the fuck do you have this? Do you have any idea what this shit does? How fucking dumb are you!?" She was shouting and swearing at him so loud it would be impossible not to hear from downstairs. But she didn't care and she couldn't control her anger. "What's the big deal? I thought you'd want to. You can't tell me you haven't before."

He tried to make light of the situation, he had even said it half-jokingly in an attempt to lighten the mood. It wasn't working. "What? You think this is what I do? You think I'm just some trashy rat who takes meth? You're unbelievable."

"Hey, what's going on?" Amanda had made her way upstairs to investigate what all the commotion was. Tyler had his back to his mum and was looking at Hannah pleadingly, but she was too angry to keep quiet. She grabbed the packet and held it up for Amanda to see. "Your precious, perfect son brought this home. Apparently it's a present for me."

Just then, Danny appeared behind Amanda, unaware of what he was about to witness. "Surprise! I'm home early!" The three of them stood in shell-shocked silence. Amanda closed her eyes, waiting for him to register what was before him. "What's going on?" he asked, sensing the tension. He glanced at Hannah's hand and she watched as his face changed from curiosity to anger. "What the fuck is that?" he asked, louder even than Hannah. Amanda gasped. Clearly it was rare for her to hear him swear. "Why don't you ask Tyler?" Hannah asked, again slamming the substance back onto the floor.

"Get out," Danny said fiercely. His order was directed at Hannah. She shook her head but followed his orders, storming out of the room and down the stairs.

"Danny, come on, be fair," she heard Amanda plead.

Hannah was too angry to think straight. She headed for the door without grabbing a single thing. She knew she couldn't go very far. She walked to the end of the street and sat on the curb.

She couldn't believe what had just happened. Of course, Danny had thought the package belonged to her. It probably hadn't helped that she had been the one holding it, but still, he hadn't even given her a chance to explain. It was so typical. And what on earth had Tyler been thinking? Did he really think that was her thing? That upset her just as much, if not more than anything else. Did he think he had to lower himself to that level to get her to like him? Was that it? That was messed up. That stuff was evil, she didn't want anything to do with it. It had been the last thing she expected him to do.

Hannah sat on the curb for what felt like an eternity, when Amanda's car pulled up in front of her.

"I'm glad you didn't go too far," was all Amanda said as she got out of the car and sat down next to her. They both sat in silence for a while.

"I'm sorry about Danny. That was uncalled for," said Amanda, breaking the silence. "I guess I should head back and grab my stuff," said Hannah. "Don't be silly. You're not going anywhere. Tyler owned up to everything. He's in big trouble," Hannah sniggered. "Right. But let me guess. I bet he's never done anything like that before."

"Well, no.."

"And I bet Danny thinks it's all my fault. I'm a bad influence. I caused him to do that."

Amanda gave her a sympathetic smile. "Look, that's probably a bit more accurate than I would like to admit." "Surprise, surprise," Hannah starred down at her feet. "What do you think?" she asked. Amanda took a deep breath. "What do *I* think? I think Tyler likes you, and I think he was trying to impress you, particularly after letting you down."

"Impress me!? I hate that stuff."

"I know you do. And don't get me wrong, I'm not trying to defend him and I'm really disappointed. He's in a lot of trouble. But from his perspective, drugs are 'cool'. At his school, the kids with drugs are the cool kids. It's really stupid, and I hate it. It scares the life out of me. But that's the way it is. And what do guys do to try and impress girls? They try to act cool. That's what he was doing. I don't think it's because he thinks you're a 'trashy rat" put it that way." Hannah lifted her head and smiled.

"You heard all that, huh?"

"Yep. But for what it's worth, I'm proud of you. I think you gave him a better serve than what I could have done. I think you got through to him more than what I could have. He's pretty embarrassed and ashamed about the whole thing."

Hannah was taken aback by Amanda. She continued to surprise her. Her son had just been found with ice, yet here she was, comforting *her* and trying to make her feel better. Shouldn't she have been acting like Danny and showing her the door? But then, she had never acted like Danny. Hannah dismissed her thoughts and brought herself back to the present. "Good. I'm glad he feels ashamed. But what about Danny? He hates me." Amanda sighed. "Danny is…a problem. He's not exactly happy about you staying. I think I've convinced him for now, but I'd recommend keeping out of his way."

Amanda looked worried and it made Hannah uneasy. She thought she could put two and two together.

"He's not going to help me, is he? Find my dad, I mean. He's not going to help me find my dad." Amanda sighed. "That's actually something I need to speak to you about. Honestly, he knows the sooner we locate your dad, the sooner you'll leave – potentially. But he's angry and he's not thinking straight right now. The short answer is 'no', he doesn't want to help you right now. I'm sure he'll calm down eventually."

"Who cares? My dad left. Maybe I don't want to find him anyway," Hannah replied gloomily, before continuing.

"They seemed so happy in the photos. Then he just took off. I bet it was because of me," Hannah let her feelings out and immediately hated herself for it. She hated that her eyes filled with tears every time she expressed her emotions. It was so childish and pathetic.

"I know there's a part of you that thinks that. But there's also a part of you that really wants to find him and I think you have to listen to that. That's where my idea comes in."

"Right. You have an idea?" asked Hannah, unconvinced. "I do.

But I don't think you're going to like it. It involves speaking to your mum."

Hannah raised her eyebrows. "Are you crazy!? *Worst idea ever!* She's never given me any information about my dad. What makes you think she's going to now? We'd have a better chance of Danny helping me."

"Not if we go about it the right way. I've met your mum, Hannah. There's something in there that we can reach. She cares about you deep down, I know it."

"Right. 'Cause you know her so well after 30 seconds. Seriously, don't waste your time."

"*Seriously* hear me out. I'm not denying you have a point. And if I show up at her door she's likely to slam it in my face. But think about it. What if I catch her out somewhere where she can't do that? There's a right way of doing this, we just have to find it, together."

Amanda looked at Hannah hopefully, but Hannah still wasn't convinced. "She's never told me a single thing about him," she said. "Right. But you never thought she had anything to tell. You thought he was a one night stand, so you never really pushed. But now you know differently. They were a couple Hannah, Leanne knows lots about him. Starting with his name. Do you know how helpful that information could be, just knowing his name? Think about it."

Amanda was excited and enthused and it continued to bewilder Hannah. After all, what was it to her if she found her dad? She barely even knew her. Why was she wasting her time with someone like her? She had to be a little crazy, Hannah decided.

CHAPTER 12

Amanda

Amanda's household was in disarray. Tyler had been grounded, Danny wasn't speaking to anyone and Hannah refused to speak to Tyler. In fact, she barely spoke at all. Amanda knew she had a lot on her mind, but she was hoping she would talk to her about it. Things had looked so promising out on the street, but she had gone back into her shell since.

As for Danny, he was furious. He couldn't believe Amanda had refused to kick Hannah out and he stomped around the house, his vein popping out of the side of his forehead. They had argued about it as Amanda defended Hannah, stating that she wasn't responsible for Tyler's actions. Danny had yelled back, telling Amanda that she was too involved with some delinquent teen instead of worrying about her own kids.

Maybe he had a point. Amanda recalled her thoughts from that eventful day and remembered she'd felt a pleather of different emotions, admittedly most of them were of concern for Hannah. Perhaps the most farfetched was the worry that Hannah was having to borrow Tyler's clothes. Not only was she out of clothes but she didn't have any nice ones. What on earth would she wear if she was ever introduced to her dad?

Amanda sighed. Yes, Danny definitely did have a point.

Still, she was in shock that Tyler had brought home drugs. She had not seen that coming. Should she have seen it coming? Had she been so caught up in helping Hannah that she'd been oblivious to her son's rebellious antics? Was she being too hard on herself? It *had* been completely out of character. But what *would* she do about Hannah's clothe situation?? She couldn't exactly go out and buy her a new wardrobe. How would Danny react to that!? He would not be impressed. Hannah probably wouldn't respond that well either. Oddly enough, material things didn't seem to impress her all that much.

Yep, this was Amanda's current train of thought. Her son had come home with ice and she was worried about Hannah's outfit! She had lost the plot.

Seeing as nobody was talking to her, Amanda had taken the free time to develop a plan for confronting Leanne. Yes, she was effectively still dedicating her time to helping Hannah. But when it came down to it, she was doing her kids a favour. Didn't she say that the sooner she found Hannah's dad the sooner she would leave? The sooner that happened the sooner things would go back to normal.

Amanda had approached Hannah with her thoughts and it had got her back talking. The two of them had decided it would be best to confront Leanne as she was leaving the Bottle-O. She was always there on the same day, at the same time. Plus it was a public place, so she would be less likely to make a scene. The bonus was they could ambush her and she didn't have the luxury of a front door to slam in her face.

Putting the final touches of the plan into action, Amanda had taken a photo of Hannah's father and placed it inside her jacket pocket. She, Hannah and Chrissie now sat outside the Donut Parlour which provided a good view of the Bottle-O that Leanne would no doubt be entering shortly. Chrissie slurped on her milkshake relatively oblivious to the plan, though Amanda sensed she knew they were up to something. Amanda had bought the girls milkshakes and doughnuts to bide some time – Chrissie was on world record pace while Hannah's food remained untouched. Amanda could tell she was uneasy and nervous. She knew Hannah didn't really think the plan would work. Amanda on the other hand was quietly confident. She was looking forward to seeing Leanne's face when she produced the photograph. Hannah had the photo album in her backpack, ready to use as part of their plan if the need presented itself. "There she is," said Hannah suddenly, peering over the top of Chrissie's head. "Who?" said Chrissie, spinning around, but Leanne was already out of sight and inside the liquor store. "Ok, here we go, are you ready Hannah?" She nodded silently. "Ready for what?" asked Chrissie, confused.

Amanda got up out of her seat and waited for Leanne to exit. As predicted, she walked out with two bottles of whisky, one in each hand. Defenceless. Amanda couldn't help but notice the bruising on Leanne's face that she had vainly attempted to hide. She chose to ignore them; for now.

"Leanne!" she yelled, stepping in front of her and blocking her path. Leanne was barely paying attention and nearly walked straight into her. "Oh, it's *you*," she said irritably, recognising her daughter's teacher. "Yes that's right. I thought I might bump into you here," she said coolly. "And what's that supposed to mean?"

Amanda didn't reply, she just looked from bottle to bottle and raised her eyebrows. Leanne huffed. "Can I help you with something? Because I really don't have time to talk to you right now."

 "Right, so you don't have time to bother finding out how your daughters are doing?"

"Oh, I'm sure they're perfectly fine. They're with you aren't they? They must be terrific," she said sarcastically. "Actually, they are terrific. I can't believe how happy they are being away from home."

"Well congratulations. Now do you mind? I have places to be."

"And I have things to discuss. Very important things." "Oh yeah, like what?"

"Like….this" Amanda reached inside her jacket and pulled out the photo. Leanne glanced at the photo and immediately turned pale. "Where did you get that?" she demanded. "Never mind that. What I'd like to know is why you've kept him a secret from Hannah?" She could tell she had caught Leanne off guard. It had been the last thing she had been expecting. She starred back at the photo. "You've been inside my house," she said accusingly. "Stop dodging the real issue here Leanne. Can you explain to me why you've been lying to your daughter?"

"This is ridiculous. You've broken into my house. This is none of your business."

"Fine. Maybe it isn't my business. I think we can both agree though, that it's definitely *her* business." Amanda signalled to Hannah and she got up out of her seat. "Hi mum," she said. She looked at the photo. "Hi *dad*," she said and glared back at Leanne. "I think she deserves some answers, don't you?"

Leanne said nothing. She was in shock and stood bewildered as Hannah began her interrogation. "You acted like you didn't even know him! How do you have photos of someone you never even knew?" said Hannah questioningly. "Here's what's going to happen," said Amanda threateningly. "I'm going to take a seat over there with Chrissie, and the two of you are going to take a seat and talk about this."

It was enough to break Leanne's silence. "And what makes you think I'm going to tell her anything?" Amanda laughed. "I don't think you really have a choice. There's some things going on in that house of yours that aren't ok. I don't know if you realise this, but as Chrissie's teacher I have a duty of care to report anything I think isn't right to child services. And to the police. Perhaps you want to think about that." Leanne shook her head. "What, so telling Hannah about her father is going to stop you from talking?"

"Yes," said Amanda, simply. "And why is that?"

"Honestly, because I'm a fair person. I'm giving you a chance here to make something right in Hannah's life. She hasn't had much of that. The least you can do is be honest with her and tell her about her biological father. You do that, and I'll take that as a step in the right direction. You do something for her and I'll do something for you. Does that sound like a deal?"

"I don't know what it is you think you're going to tell anyone."

"Oh really? So you're happy for me to contact the police then?" Leanne just looked at her with daggers. "You really do have some nerve, lady."

"So, that's a deal then?" Amanda stood her ground. "Fine," said Leanne. "Right then, you two have a nice chat. Hannah, if you have any problems, you know I'm right here, ok?"

"Thanks," replied Hannah weakly.

Hannah

"I can't believe you've been living with that woman," said Leanne in disbelief as Amanda sat at the table with Chrissie. "I can't believe you didn't tell me about my dad." Leanne put the two whisky bottles on the table and sat down. "So you think you're just going to threaten me into speaking?"
"That was pretty much the plan, yeah."
Leanne sighed. "Well, 'it's a long story."
"I figured. Mum, you know I've got the whole album right? I'm not stupid. You two were together for ages." "So it's you who's been in the house? That time the doorbell went. The time Dale went…" Leanne stopped herself. Hannah could tell she was reliving that afternoon. Hannah didn't want to think about what had happened when she had left. Instead, she grabbed the album out from her backpack. "Good God," whispered Leanne as Han-

nah flicked through the pages. "You know I have so many questions. When did you meet? Where did you meet? What's his name? Why did he leave? Was it because of me?" Hannah rushed the last question. Perhaps she didn't really want to know the answer to that one. Leanne skipped the first two questions. "He didn't leave me, I left him. And I suppose it was because of you, but I was young and stupid and it was such a long time ago."

Hannah didn't quite understand her mum's explanation. Did that mean Leanne had left him because he didn't want a baby? "So he *does* know I exist. That's why you left?" Leanne shook her head. "Then why did you leave?"

"No, he doesn't know about you, Hannah." Hannah sat in silence as she let that fact sink in. She found herself once again blinking back the tears. So her dad didn't know she existed. '*No wonder he's never tried to find me,*' she thought. Looking at the photos seemed to have had a similar effect on Leanne; she was teary too.

She re-composed herself and glared at her daughter. "So how much more do I have to tell you before you go back to that nosey woman?"
Hannah didn't hold back. "I want to know why you left him. What was wrong with him? God knows he couldn't be worse than Dale, and you've stuck with *him*." Leanne sighed.
"There wasn't anything wrong with him," Leanne paused and then continued. Hannah was surprised by how much she let out, given her years of silence.
"I freaked out when I fell pregnant. He was so different to me. And we were both so young. He was so career driven. All I wanted to do was run my parents' bakery. I always felt inferior to him, like I'd just hold him back. I knew his parents thought as much. And then I found out I was pregnant. He'd just told me his big plans. He was going to study overseas and he wanted me to come with him. He was going to be a doctor or I don't know, a physio or something. If I told him I was pregnant I was scared

he'd stay and I'd ruin his career. So I left him. Maybe I should have given him the choice, but like he really had one anyway. His parents would have made him stay away and I didn't want to put it on him. Anyway, I had you and I continued with the bakery. I was so busy I almost forgot about him. Then I met Dale."

"Then you met Dale," repeated Hannah glumly. "But I have more questions. What was his name? Where did you go? How did you just leave, what did you say to him?"

Leanne starred off into the distance. She sighed. "Hannah, I've done a lot of things I'm not proud of," she looked down at her hands. "No kidding," said Hannah without hiding her sarcasm. Her comment didn't sit well with her mother.

"Look, I don't know what you want me to say. You come here and demand answers with that stupid, ridiculous woman and just expect me to lay it all out for you, it's not that simple."

"Why didn't you just tell me?" Hannah asked bluntly. Leanne glanced across at her daughter. How was she meant to explain why she hadn't told her daughter about her biological father? The truth was, it upset her to even think about him. Memories of her old boyfriend reminded her of a time when she had truly been happy. The mistake hadn't been falling pregnant, her error had been walking away. And in brutal fashion. But she wouldn't make herself re-live that. No threat was going to make her go down that road. She continued to stare at her daughter, contemplating how much to say. She was overcome with a wave of emotions. She felt ambushed, angry and upset, yet a part of her wanted to get it all off her chest and confide in Hannah. Maybe she did owe her the truth, at least part of it.

She had never expected that she would be here, in these circumstances, telling her daughter about her biggest regrets. Yet here she was, without much choice.

 "Because I was ashamed. I've been such a lousy mother Hannah. These photos are just a reminder of all the wrong choices I made. And I don't mean you. I don't know how to explain it. But sometimes I look at you and you're just a reminder of all the things… we were so happy." She sniffed again. The two of them sat in silence. Hannah was taking in all this new information. At least some of it made sense now. The reasons her mum had been so cold towards Hannah, the years of bitterness and neglect had all stemmed from an immense feeling of guilt. Hannah hadn't done anything wrong, except for being born. And Dale had only contributed to the bitter feelings, made worse when Chrissie had come along. Hannah was just a painful reminder of the life Leanne could have had if she hadn't walked away. '*All the wrong choices*,' thought Hannah.

"I should never have stayed with Dale," Leanne said, breaking the silence. "But then I fell pregnant with Chrissie and I couldn't do it on my own again. So I stayed. I lived with so many regrets, it's ironic really. I stayed with Dale because I regretted leaving Ethan and now Dale is the biggest regret of all." The tears ran silently down Leanne's cheek.

 "Ethan?" Hannah asked suddenly. Leanne smiled. It had been so long since Hannah had seen her mum smile. It made such a difference, even though her face was worn and tired. "Your dad's name was Ethan. Ethan Stephenson. I used to call him 'Even Stevens'. We met at a party. It was after we'd finished High School, though he was a year older. He was actually one of my friend's brothers. I remember I'd made my chocolate blueberry muffins for the party and he ate about half of them! That's how we got talking, he loved my bloody choc-blueberry muffins." She starred past Hannah, lost in thought. "They were my favourite," said Hannah. "I know they were," Leanne looked back at Hannah and gave a sad smile. "You two probably have a lot in common." Her smile faded. Hannah starred at her mum sadly. "I'm sorry. I know I shouldn't have kept this from you. I can't believe I'm telling you about it now, after all this time."

 "There's a lot of things we don't speak about, isn't there?" said Hannah. Leanne just looked at her daughter and said nothing. Hannah knew it was a face full of guilt. Hannah could feel her rollercoaster of emotions get the better of her. She swayed from feeling sad and sympathetic to angry and betrayed. She had wanted answers for so long and it had only taken a threat to call the police from a stranger to get her to talk. "You should have told me. The number of times I used to ask you, you made out like he was nothing to you. But you know so much. Did you ever think I might want to meet him?" Hannah was raising her voice now but she couldn't help it. "I know you did. But I didn't want you to. For selfish reasons. I'm sorry…"

"Sorry doesn't really cut it. I've been living like this without a dad, and you've made me live with that creep. Now look at you. You can't keep pretending everything's ok. We both know it's not."

Hannah was surprising herself. She'd never told her mum what she really thought. Most of the time her mum was too off her face to care, or even take in what she was saying. Amanda had been right in deciding to confront her here. It was probably the only time her mum was sober. "I don't know what to say, I know I haven't been a good mum." Hannah shrugged her shoulders. "If you're expecting me to comfort you and tell you that isn't true, think again. Because you haven't been a good mum. You used to be, before *he* came along. But not anymore."

Hannah said it so matter-of-factly she could tell that it had cut her mum deep. But she didn't care. She needed to hear it, finally. It felt so good to get it off her chest and tell her how she was feeling. No more cover ups. It didn't do anyone any favours. "I can't believe you didn't even give him a choice. He doesn't even know he has a daughter. All this time." Leanne wiped the tears from her face and rubbed her nose. Hannah wished she would stop crying. Her emotional ride would no doubt swing back to sympathetic if she wasn't careful. "You know I want to meet him, right? That's why we showed you the photo." Leanne continued to look upset. "I wish I could help you. But I honestly don't know where he is. I haven't seen him in 15 years."

"The only reason you've decided you want to help me is so Amanda doesn't go running to the police. You know, that *ridiculous woman's* done more for me in like a week than you've done in 10 years."

Hannah continued with the brutality and Leanne attempted to defend herself. "It's not all my fault you know. Dale doesn't exactly make things easy."

 "Right, and who brought Dale into the picture? I can't believe you let him get away with the shit he does." "What am I supposed to do?"

"You know, all this time I thought it was best to keep what he does a secret, pretend it doesn't happen. But what good does that do, really? It just makes things worse. It makes *him* worse. If you spoke up, maybe he'd disappear and things would go back to normal."

 "I don't think it's that simple Hannah. Besides, I'm not all roses myself. What would happen to you and Chrissie?"

"Who knows, maybe we'd finally get help. Anything would be better than what we live with right now. You're just a coward." Hannah was being harsh, but her mum deserved to feel bad. '*Give her a taste of her own medicine,*' thought Hannah. Leanne looked across at Amanda with her younger daughter.

"How is Chrissie doing?" she asked. Hannah shrugged. "Honestly, I don't know. You know, I don't know what's worse; growing up without a dad who is probably a decent person, or living with a *dad* who's an absolute dead beat. Jesus, she's probably more messed up than I am." Leanne looked defeated. "I really am sorry. I don't know how to fix this."

"You could start by ending it with Dale."

"It's not that simple. And he's not always like this, and I, I got in his way, I shouldn't have done that."

"Don't you dare defend him. Nobody deserves that mum, nobody. Then again, you said I deserve what I got. You're always defending that piece of shit, that's half the problem." Leanne looked disgruntled by Hannah's last comment. "I think I've said just about all I need to say," she said and made to get up out of her chair. "Oh, that'd be right mum, go ahead and leave when things get a bit hard. You're good at that."

Amanda

Amanda sat with Chrissie, watching closely and trying to listen in to the conversation a few tables away. Chrissie was no longer distracted by her milkshake and was proving to be a distraction herself.
"What are they doing? Why does mummy look so upset?" she asked. Amanda didn't really know what to say, so she didn't say anything.
"Is it about Hannah's Dad? It is isn't it?"
'*Kids these days*,' thought Amanda. There was just no getting anything passed them.
"Yes, it is Chrissie. They're just trying to sort some things out. But you have nothing to worry about ok?"
Chrissie looked upset.
"She's going to find him, and then she's going to leave," her eyes welled up. "Chrissie, no that's not it. She'd never leave you don't be silly. She just wants to find out who he is, that's all. There's a lot of things your mum can help her with, they just need to have a chat, ok?" Amanda didn't know how well she was reassuring her, Chrissie seemed convinced that her sister was going to disappear.
Just then Amanda noticed Leanne get up to leave, but she sat down again. Perhaps this was her call to intervene.
"Come on Chrissie, let's see how they're going."
The two of them got up and made their way over to Hannah and Leanne.

"So, has the deal been met?" Amanda asked.

"I guess. I got a name at least. Ethan Stephenson. He's a year older than mum, he was my mum's friend's brother, he's a doctor or a physio and he likes my mum's muffins. But he's probably overseas somewhere." Hannah summed up the conversation and Leanne raised her eyebrows in surprise, clearly taken aback by all the information she'd absorbed.

Hannah had done well. It was definitely something to work with, a full name was significant progress on its own. Not that it was an unusual name, but still, it was something to go on.

"So are the three of you going to leave me now?" Asked Leanne a little aggressively.

"Well, I would have thought that was up to you," said Amanda. Hannah looked at Amanda, puzzled.

"Well yes, I guess it's up to you as well, and you too Chrissie," Amanda added.

"I'm not setting foot in that house if *he's* there."

"Actually, he's not home. He went fishing for the week. Possibly longer."

"Fishing!?" Hannah snorted. "Is that what you're calling it now?"

"That's what he told me. He took his rod," Leanne added, as if that confirmed it.

Hannah rolled her eyes. "You really are delusional."

"So you're going to go back with her then?" asked Leanne, a little put out.

"What's it to you? You've never cared about where I go or who I stay with before. And what makes you think I want to come home?"

Leanne looked at Amanda. Was it desperation Amanda could see in her eyes? Amanda couldn't believe it.

"Leanne, could I speak with you – privately, for a minute?"

Leanne crossed her arms while Hannah made to object. "This will only take a minute Hannah."

Hannah sighed and took Chrissie back to her seat.

Amanda turned to Leanne. "I've got to say, Hannah has a point. What gives?"

Leanne still had her arms folded. "I don't know who you think you are or why you think I have to justify myself to you, but Hannah obviously respects you, so…" "So her opinion matters to you?" asked Amanda, unconvinced. "Because I'm a little confused here. One minute you couldn't care less about Hannah, or Chrissie for that matter. Suddenly I threaten police intervention and you want Hannah back. Do you honestly care about her, or are you more worried about an investigation? Tell me Leanne, which one is it?"

Leanne glared at Amanda with as much hate as she could muster. She didn't want to admit what she was feeling, but Amanda's tactic was working.

"I haven't been the best parent ok, fine I'll admit that. So maybe I can make it up to Hannah, I don't know, maybe together we could find out a bit more…"

"If I didn't know better," Amanda paused for affect. "I don't think you want to do this just to 'make it up to Hannah'. I think there's a big part of you that wants to find him too."

Leanne really did hate this woman. How did she know? And how the hell had Hannah managed to get her involved in all this?

CHAPTER 13

Hannah

Hannah didn't know how to feel about going home as she sat in Amanda's car on the way back to her house. She had gathered her backpack and clothes and had left in a rush without really knowing if she would return or even if she would see Tyler again. As angry as she still was with him she knew she would miss him. Going back home was the last place she wanted to be. And yet, going back gave her a small sense of hope. It might be her biggest chance of finding answers and ultimately, locating her dad. Her mum had already opened up to her more than she had expected. All she needed was to keep digging.

Still, she wasn't sure how her mum would cope. Amanda had confiscated her whisky bottles like she was one of her students and replaced them with cash. Hannah didn't know if that was a smart move. She didn't like the idea of her mum thinking she could get her hands on easy money. But at least Amanda had taken the alcohol away. The deal was that Leanne would use the money to purchase proper groceries for the three of them. Hannah was to call Amanda each night at exactly 6.00pm to report on how she and her sister were going. If Hannah didn't call, Amanda would pay a visit, and if there was no answer she would call the police. The same would apply if Chrissie didn't show up at school.

Amanda had also arranged secret code words with Hannah so that if she felt unsafe she could use them during her 6.00pm call or via text. She had even shown Chrissie how to use Hannah's phone and call or text Amanda if required, just as a precaution.

Hannah sighed as Amanda pulled up outside her house. It looked more gloomy and shabby than ever before. Amanda looked across at her. "This doesn't have to be permanent ok? If for one minute you don't feel right, you just remember what we discussed and I'll be here in a heartbeat. We're going to find him, I promise."

"Don't," said Hannah. "Don't make promises you don't know if you can keep." She said it a little too harshly and chose not to say anything else. It definitely wasn't how she had planned on thanking Amanda for all her help. She just didn't know how to say it. She'd never had much to be thankful for.

"Ok, well, stay safe you two. I'll speak to you at 6.00pm, and Chrissie, I'll see you tomorrow!" Hannah and Chrissie got out of the car. Amanda got out too, she stood awkwardly, not really knowing what to do. She hung by her car as Hannah and Chrissie approached the front door.

Leanne opened it and Hannah stepped inside. Chrissie waved to Amanda and Leanne closed the door behind them.

Hannah took a look around and felt uneasy. Any ounce of happiness she'd had seeped out of her as the realisation of being back home hit her hard.

Leanne greeted them both, her hands full with groceries. "I've been shopping! I bought you some stuff. I was, err, going to make my muffins but I forgot a heap of ingredients! I've bought all this though instead!" She was being over-enthusiastic and it sickened Hannah. It couldn't have been more fake. Not to mention she was fidgety and itchy. She was clearly having withdrawals. Hannah had a quick look through the bags of groceries. It looked like she would be back to eating microwaved meals and toasted sandwiches. She hadn't even bought anything nice to put on the bread. "All you've bought us is the bare minimum mum, would it have killed you to buy some sauce to have with the pasta? At least 'mac and cheese' has cheese, so you did well there," she said sarcastically. There was no Dale around to hit her for being 'bad-mannered'.

Leanne shook her head at her daughter. "Well I'm soooorry your meals aren't 5 star like you've been having at that bloody Queen's house. How about if you don't like it, don't eat it."

"I'm just trying to figure out how you've only managed this crappy food when I saw how much money you got. Where's the rest of it?"

"What are you, my mother? There's a whole week's worth of food there Hannah, don't be so ungrateful." Her tone was childish and defensive. Hannah scoffed at her mum and headed to her bedroom. She was meant to be attempting to get along, but all she felt like doing was arguing with her. It wasn't exactly the best approach to finding out more about her dad, but she couldn't help it. Her mum was pathetic, and it if wasn't so frustrating it would have been sad. On top of it all, her room still smelt funny and her bed still somehow felt damp.

Chrissie appeared in Hannah's doorway as she stood starring at her bed in disgust. "Daddy's definitely not here," she said, satisfied. It used to kill Hannah that Chrissie felt so lovingly about her evil father, but the fact she was now scared of him upset her a whole lot more. Chrissie plonked herself down on Hannah's bed, oblivious to the bad smell and dampness.

Amanda

Amanda's house felt empty and so did she. She couldn't quite understand how a girl who said so little could be so noticeably absent, and yet, the household itself had been affected. Jenna was lonely without Chrissie, Danny still wasn't speaking to Tyler, or Amanda for that matter, which was making it all the more difficult for Amanda to get anywhere with Hannah's dad. She had 'googled' his name but hadn't found anything significant. She had also tried Facebook but the name Ethan Stephenson was even more common than she had predicted. She needed something more specific; a date of birth; an occupation.

The last time she had spoken to Hannah she had asked her to find out more – what was his sister's name – where did she live? What did she do? Hannah had sounded as flat and distant as ever and it bothered Amanda a little bit. It also annoyed her. She could be so close to finding her father, why wasn't she doing her best to try?

Tyler had also been acting funny since Hannah had left. He was grounded and he shut himself in his room without saying a word to anyone. He seemed annoyed at both his parents – he had become protective of Hannah and couldn't understand why they had let her go back home. It hadn't exactly reassured Amanda who still felt uneasy about the whole thing. It potentially hadn't been the wisest decision, or the safest. But it was definitely the best chance of finding as much information as possible, particularly when Danny wasn't having any involvement. Plus, it meant Jenny might stop looking over her shoulder and wondering what was going on.

At least the nightly phone calls meant Amanda could keep track of Hannah and make sure she was ok. Plus, Chrissie had been showing up to school each day and had seemed in relatively good spirits. The most frustrating thing was that it had been nearly a week and she had made no progress. Of course she hadn't been expecting to find him in such a short space of time, but she had been expecting to find something!

There was something stopping Hannah from speaking to her mum. Or perhaps she still didn't trust Amanda enough with personal information. Either way, maybe it was time for Amanda to try a new tactic. She had a feeling there was someone else who she might be able to open up to.

 Amanda made her way up the stairs and knocked on Tyler's door. "I'm not hungry," he answered. "Just as well, your dinner isn't ready."

"Leave me alone then." Amanda rolled her eyes at the door. *'Teenage boys,'* she thought to herself. "I have a favour to ask."

"Ask Jenna."

"Ty, stop being ridiculous and open the door."
"Leave me alone."
"You know, it's not my fault this happened. You're the one who brought drugs into the house. If you hadn't, dad probably wouldn't have kicked Hannah and Chrissie out."
Silence, and then, the sound of the door handle.
"I told him that had nothing to do with Hannah. He's a friggin' idiot."
"Maybe. Now, can you do me a favour or not?"
Tyler had clearly been expecting a lecture or even a penalty for calling his dad an idiot. The fact that Amanda chose to ignore it seemed to calm him down.
"What is it?"
"I need you to speak to Hannah for me."
"Pfft, like she wants to speak to me. She didn't even say goodbye."
"Well, now's her chance. I think she'll be happy to hear your voice."
"Now I think *you're* an idiot," he said with a smile.
"Don't push it," she said and handed him her phone.
"What do I say?"
"'Hello? How are you'? That's always a good place to start."
"Har, har. I mean, what do you want me to say? Why do you want me to speak to her?"
"Because I can't get through to her. It's like, I don't know. She's so close I think it's scared her. She just needs someone to talk to, and I don't think that someone is me."
"And what makes you think it's me?"
"She talks to you. She tells you things. At least give it a go?"
"Fine. So what do I say?"
"I don't know, just talk to her. Have a conversation, she'll come 'round."
"But I don't even know what you want to find out?"
"I think that's the best part. Just be yourself," she smiled and headed down the stairs. She stopped half way down so she could listen in on the conversation. Of course, she could only hear

Tyler's half of it.

"Hello?"

"Yeah it's Tyler."

"I just thought I'd say hello. See what you were doing?"

"No, I'm not doing that. That was dumb, I'm sorry."

"Yeah, I am. I didn't want you to leave. But I mean, maybe you'll be able to find him now."

"Well it would be easier if you just asked."

"Yeah you're right, I don't know much. Except she probably really wants to tell you, deep down. I know I would if I had a secret like that."

"Why not?"

"Like mother like daughter then, huh?"

"I mean you're stubborn too. And you're scared."

"Well why else aren't you trying to find answers then?"

"Just ask her."

"So, what else are you doing? What's Chrissie doing – Jenna wants to know? Tell her Jenna misses her."

"I don't know, I'm grounded."

"Because I told him they were mine, not yours."

"Yeah, I guess. He's being a pain."

"If you say so."

"Your dad probably cares about you too. Guess you'll never know."

"Anyway, maybe we can hang out sometime."

"Yeah, when I'm not grounded."

"Ok, enjoy dinner. Nah she didn't want to speak to you."

"Ok, see ya."

Tyler hung up and Amanda raced down the stairs, not wanting him to know she'd been eavesdropping.

Tyler followed her down the stairs and handed her back her phone. "So, how'd you go?" Amanda asked innocently. "Who knows? She's being stubborn. I reckon she's just doing it to be difficult. She seemed pretty happy I was grounded though," he smiled. "Well, thanks for trying. Dinner's not far away, you can set the table."

*

It appeared that Amanda's new tactic had done the job, or, effectively, Tyler had done the job. She sat by her desk consumed by her thoughts as her students practised writing their names. She had to laugh at herself for encouraging Tyler to talk to Hannah in the first place. She had an idea most parents wouldn't want their sons to have anything to do with a girl who had influenced their child to take drugs. The irony of it was that Hannah hadn't actually done any influencing, in fact she hated everything about them. Amanda's ignorant son hadn't been aware of that and it did scare her a little bit that he had got his hands on them so easily. She did take comfort that he had showed remorse and above anything she'd been surprised and impressed by Hannah's reaction. She wished those around her could see that side of her. It seemed most of her teachers had come to the conclusion that she was trouble, an assumption that was made purely on a stereotype. Of course, Hannah wasn't completely innocent. Amanda knew she gave her teachers a hard time. Still, it hadn't taken Amanda long too break down her walls, admittedly with some help, and she unscrunched the note Chrissie had given to her 'from Hannah' 2 minutes earlier.

She had jotted down a handful of notes in dot point form in response to Amanda's latest questions.

Sister's Name: Michelle Stephenson (possibly married – was engaged to a rich Italian guy 'Chris Genit-something')
Age: Same age as mum
Living: not sure – probably stayed in Melbourne

It wasn't anything substantial, but still, it could be useful. Amanda shoved the note in her pocket, making herself a mental note to check the internet on lunch break, when she caught sight of Chrissie slumped on a bean bag, starring miserably out the window.

Amanda approached her. "Chrissie are you ok? Has anything happened at home? Is Hannah ok?"

"She's fine. Not everything is about Hannah you know." Chrissie folder her arms underneath her and continued to stare out the window. Her response caught Amanda off guard. "Of course it's not. I'm sorry Chrissie, why are you so upset?"

Chrissie wiped her eyes on her arm. "All my flowers are dead." Amanda had to rack her brains. What flowers was she talking about? And then it came to her and she felt sick to the stomach. She had forgotten all about the dandelions she had asked Chrissie to collect.

"Why did you get me to pick so many flowers if you were just going to let them die?" Tears were streaking down her face now and Amanda felt horrible. How could she have been so thoughtless? She had been so caught up in Hannah's troubles that she had completely forgotten about the activity she had planned. Not that she'd exactly had an activity planned. She had meant to think of something later.

Had she been neglecting the rest of her students? Most likely. She needed to pull herself together. She was a teacher, responsible for her students. She wasn't responsible for Hannah, as much as she wanted to think otherwise.

"I'm so sorry Chrissie. I am the world's worst teacher! Maybe we can still use them, I'll see what I can do."

"No, don't worry. I don't even care about the flowers." She got up off her bean bag, rubbed her eyes on her dress and made her way to her desk. "And you're not the world's worst teacher. You're just not a very good gardener." Amanda had to stifle a laugh at this statement. "You have a point there," she said with a smile. It was definitely a wakeup call. Jenny would still be suspicious if she started neglecting her students.

It did make her worry about Chrissie, though. The poor girl had been through so much in the past couple of weeks. Not only had she lost her hero, she was now faced with the fear of losing her sister too. Not to mention she would have noticed a change in her mum as well. On top of all this, she was no longer the centre of attention at home. Without her dad around and the mission of finding Hannah's real dad, Chrissie had no doubt seeped into the background. Changes as big as these would be hard enough for anyone to take, let alone a 5 year old.

Amanda spent the rest of the afternoon reading to her class while they lied down on the floor. It had been a while since she had let her brain switch off and it felt good to let go for a while. She took the moment to enjoy the peace and quiet as the majority of her students began to drift off to sleep.

*

Hannah called promptly at 5.55pm.

"Hi Hannah, how was your day?"

"Fine, did you get my note?"

"Yes, I did thank you."

"Is any of it helpful?"

"Possibly. I haven't had a chance to have a look yet."

"Oh ok. I just wanted to give it to you in case I forgot."

"Yeah, no worries. I've just had a busy day. And I'm a bit concerned about Chrissie. I think she's feeling a bit left out. Maybe it would be a good idea if you took a break from pestering your mum and spent some time with your sister?"

A pause.

"So, let me get this straight? One minute you're on my back for not asking questions and now you're telling me to back off?"

"Just for a couple of days. Chrissie isn't coping. And you're not the only one whose been neglecting her. I had her in tears today and I feel awful!"

"Ok fine. I'll leave mum alone. I don't know how much more I can ask her anyway, it took me ages just to get her to remember her friend's name! She's lost way too many brain cells." Hannah fell silent.

"Well, a name is a start. I'll let you know how I go."

"Ok. Cool. Say hi to Tyler."

"Actually he's here. Did you want to say hi yourself?"

"Um, sure ok."

"Not for too long though ok, he is still grounded you know," Amanda joked and handed Tyler the phone.

He grabbed it and headed up to his bedroom. She had felt him lingering and sensed he was hoping he might be able to have a chat. She hadn't noticed that Danny was also lingering.

"So, you've found out some details about Hannah's dad?" he asked.

"Yeah, I have. It's not a lot to go on, especially not for me with limited resources. But it's a start I guess."

"What have you got?"

Amanda looked at him eagerly. "Does this mean you're going to help?" she asked hopefully.

"Depends if you have anything worth investigating," he replied.

Amanda dug into her pocket and pulled out her note from Hannah.

"Here. This is some information on his sister. Her dad's name is Ethan Stephenson, he's a year older than Leanne, he was studying to be a physiotherapist, or something like that, he might have moved overseas and…"

"Ok, honey slow down! It's probably going to be more helpful if you write all that down."

"Ok great. So what's with the sudden change of mind?"

Danny shrugged his shoulders. "You're letting Tyler break the rules by allowing him to talk to her. It seems you're hell bent on helping her whether I like it or not. I figured I might as well see what I can do or you're not going to get anywhere. I don't know how long I can live like this, so the sooner I can get this sorted the better," he gave her a hug and she curled herself in his arms.

She knew he would come around.

*

Danny worked tirelessly and spent many hours in front of his laptop after work for the next few nights. She even heard him making the odd phone call, trying to establish connections with people who could point him in the right direction.

Amanda was delighted that he'd changed his mind and had finally decided to help. She wondered if he was feeling guilty about sending Hannah back home. Hopefully he had come to the realisation that Tyler's antics weren't actually her fault. Whatever the reason, Amanda was extremely grateful. Plus, it was nice to have things back to normal between them. They so rarely fought and she couldn't handle it when they didn't speak. Their fights never usually lasted long on the rare occasion that they eventuated.

They would normally argue, say what they had to say and then literally kiss and make up.

The thought of a fight ending in physicality had never even crossed her mind. It was strange how Hannah coming into her life had changed the way she saw things.

Now, she couldn't help but wonder what sort of fights Hannah witnessed at home. These thoughts were met with a feeling of remorse as Amanda questioned if she was doing the right thing. Should she at the very least be raising her concerns with Jenny, instead of hiding them and taking matters into her own hands? Should she be considering contacting Child Services? Should she be doing more to encourage Leanne to speak out? Seek help? A part of her knew she should be answering 'yes' to some, if not all of these questions, yet she was obeying Hannah's wishes to stay silent. She thought she was doing Hannah a favour by helping her find her father, but deep down she knew the biggest favour she could do was to get her proper help. Get her out of that house!

Amanda sighed to herself and wondered if she would ever find a second when her thoughts didn't revert to Hannah. What on earth used to occupy her before they met!?

If she was looking for a 'Hannah free' moment, it would have to wait as Danny strode into the house after work with a strut in his step. He didn't even kiss her hello. He was much too proud of himself. "We've got him" he said as though he was a detective and had found his suspect. He placed a handful of documents on the kitchen table. "Actually, we've got both of them. We found his sister too. Turns out her husband is none other than Christopher Genitsopolous" he paused for effect. Amanda raised her eyebrows. "Who?" she asked. "Oh, he's a pretty big name in Real Estate. Our Firm's dealt with him a few times. He's done pretty well for himself. He was caught up in a pretty big lawsuit a couple of years ago. He won the case. It was massive. Anyway, she works in administration in the city part time. Not that she'd need to. He's raking it in."

"Right. And what about Ethan?"

"Take a look for yourself. Seems pretty standard."

Amanda grabbed the documents from the bench and flicked through the pages. Most of the information was regarding Chris. Finally she came to the page on Ethan. "He's a chiropractor! Hah! Physio, chiro, same thing." she kept reading. "And he's based in Sydney! No home address?"

"Well he owns the Chiro he works at, so you can contact them directly." Amanda raised her eyebrows again. "He owns it? Wow, he must be doing pretty well too." "You could say that. Anyway his office contact number is listed at the bottom. I've got Michelle's work number too, just in case."

"This is unreal. Hannah's going to be stoked!"

Danny changed his tone, a concerned look on his face.

"Yeah, look I probably wouldn't mention any of this to her until you've spoken to her dad first."

"Really? But she's going to call any minute!"

"Then I'd suggest you keep it brief. There's a good chance he'll want nothing to do with her. It's going to be a pretty huge shock. And she's 15 not 2. He's got a life now, you know."

"Gee, thanks Mr Optimism!"

"Look, I don't want to spoil the good news. I'm just being realistic and preparing you for the worst. To me, it looks like he's got his life together. Just be ready is all I'm saying. The kid's going to feel pretty flat if she finds out her dad wants nothing to do with her." Amanda opened her mouth to argue, but stopped herself. The fact that he was thinking about Hannah's feelings was a nice change, and she chose to bite her tongue in case she said the wrong thing.

Anyway, Danny did have a point. Hannah had been through enough. It was definitely better to wait and speak to Ethan first.

Amanda couldn't contain her excitement and did her best to hide her emotion when she received her 6.00pm call from Hannah. She kept the conversation brief and barely even listened to what Hannah had to say. She hung up the phone with a sigh of relief and continued to relive her conversation with Danny. She couldn't believe he had actually done it. He'd found Hannah's dad. Her next dilemma was how exactly she was going to break the news to Ethan. He lived in Sydney, a whole state away. Was she meant to fly up there and turn up at his work? Was it simply just a phone call? A phone call didn't seem right. Plus, he probably wouldn't believe her. Maybe she could call to set up a meeting? She had never thought this far ahead. Now that she'd finally come to this point, she had no plan.

*

After a restless sleep and her mind racing, Amanda awoke with a new idea. Ethan's sister. Wouldn't it be best to receive this kind of news from a family member? Besides, she had been friends with Leanne, maybe she could help get things moving.

She grabbed Michelle and Ethan's details, got Tyler and Jenna ready and hopped in the car. Once alone, she pulled into the staff car park and gathered her thoughts. As much as the news coming from Michelle had seemed like a good idea, the thought of speaking to Hannah's dad directly was far more thrilling. Plus, she would be able to read his tone and gain a sense of how he was taking the news. She looked at her phone, her thumb hovering over the little green telephone icon, feeling all kinds of crazy. 'Let's do this' she said, encouraging herself.

She took a deep breath and pressed down, dialling Ethan's office. She lifted her phone to her ear, the anticipation making her heart race. "Even Stevens Chiropractors, how can I help you?"

"Er, hi. I was after Ethan Stephenson."

"I'm sorry, he's out of the office today. Did you need to book an appointment?"

"Um, no, not exactly. Could you put me through to his mobile?"

"I'm sorry, he's not contactable on his mobile today. Can I take a message?"

"Do you know when he'll be back?"

"He's due back on Monday. Is there something I can help you with?"

Amanda sighed, that was too far away. "No, that's ok. I'll call back on Monday. Thanks, bye."

She hung up. Could she wait until Monday? That was practically a week away!

She dug into her handbag and pulled out Michelle's office number. 'Looks like its Plan B. Or was it Plan A'? Was calling his sister really such a good idea? What would she think?

Could she give her a try? Was that beyond ridiculous!?

Without really knowing what to say, she dialled the number.

"Hi, can I please speak to Michelle Genitsopolous?"

"One moment, can I ask whose calling?"

"It's, um, Amanda Carson," she said awkwardly. "One moment."

Before Amanda had time to compose herself, she was speaking to Hannah's aunty.

"Hello, Michelle speaking. Sorry, who's this?"

"My name is Amanda Carson. I'm really sorry to bother you but I'm trying to get in contact with your brother, Ethan."

"Ok? Are you one of his patients? He's at a conference…"

"No, I'm not a patient. This is regarding something else. Sorry, I shouldn't be bothering you at work. It's about Leanne Thompson." Amanda held her breath. A moment's pause and then…" What do you want with that whore?"

Amanda was speechless. Of all the bizarre scenarios that had played out in her head, she hadn't been expecting that.

"Sorry?"

"If you're referring to the same Leanne Thompson who ripped my brother's heart out and then never spoke to her best friend again, yeah, I'd like to know what you want with her and why you're involving my brother."

Amanda was completely caught off guard. "I'm sorry, I wasn't aware of anything like that. I think there's been a misunderstanding. I'm very sorry to bother you." "Maybe you should speak to Jack Gardiner. I'm sure he can fill you in. Have a nice day." the line disconnected.

What on earth had just happened?! And who the hell was Jack Gardiner?

 As 6.00pm drew closer Amanda was still totally confused. She didn't know what to think. And despite Danny's advice she was now considering filling Hannah in. She needed to know who this Jack person was, and also what it might mean. Michelle had led her down a new path. A path that questioned if in fact Ethan really was Hannah's father. And as much as that might hurt Hannah, she deserved the truth.

CHAPTER 14

Hannah

Hannah hadn't been making much progress with her mum. She seemed depressed and wasn't coping at all with having no alcohol in the house. She was starting to take it out on Hannah too. It had the effect of changing Hannah's mindset, making her more determined to find as much information about her dad as possible. It was just extremely difficult to get this information out of someone who was so down and so angry. On the other hand, she was trying to be a bit more discrete with how she went about it. She was trying to follow Amanda's wishes and not say too much in front of Chrissie.

The only positive was that it had been nearly two weeks since Dale had been home, which meant Hannah was no longer on edge. Leanne wasn't coping too well without him though, which only upset Hannah more. She couldn't work out what her mum missed most, her low life boyfriend or his evil drugs. He seemed like a drug himself. Leanne knew he was no good for her, yet she craved him anyway. Hannah was finding herself counting down the minutes until her phone call with Amanda, hoping she might have news. Hannah knew that it was highly unlikely, she hadn't really given her much to go on. If anything, Amanda had seemed a little distant and Hannah wondered if it was simply because she had no news to share. She was probably sick of Hannah and her annoying daily calls. Hannah also guessed it might have something to do with Danny. She figured he would probably be trying to stop her from taking the call. Nonetheless, as the clock ticked over 6, she made her regular call.

"Hey Hannah, how was your day?"

"Yeah, ok"

"Great, so um. I have news. Kind of big news. But not great news. But news"

"Ok… what is it?"

"So, Danny found your dad's sister."

"His sister? Why was he trying to find his sister?"

"Because the more leads we have the better. Anyway, I spoke to her."

"Ok…and…"

"She didn't seem that happy with your mum. She ah, called her a whore in fact."

"Ok… did she say why?"

"Well no, not exactly. But um, I think you need to ask your mum one more question."

"Like why my aunty thinks she's a whore?"

"Or, you could ask her who Jack Gardiner is."

"Who?"

"Jack Gardiner. That was Michelle's clue."

"Who is he?"

"Like I said, I think that might be a question for your mum."

Hannah hung up the phone. Her insides were aching and she felt faint. Did this mean what she thought it meant? Timed to perfection, Leanne entered the room. "Well, that was short and sweet. Not much to talk about then?"

"Who the fuck is Jack Gardiner?" Hannah couldn't control her outburst, her mind was racing.

Leanne looked at her daughter, clearly taken aback. She paused, her mind ticking over. "Don't try to think of something smart. Who is he?"

"Don't speak to me like that, Hannah."

"Answer the question. Is he my dad?"

"What!? God no, of course not."

"Well, why does Ethan's sister think you're a whore, and why did she mention his name?"

Leanne was silent as she let the information sink in. "Michelle? When did you speak to her?"

"I didn't. Amanda did. She found her. Who is he?"

"Hannah, I'd really rather not go there. It's not something I'm proud of."

"Well, no shit. You slept with him, didn't you? You cheated on dad with him. Or is this Jack guy actually my dad?"

"I told you he isn't. And everyone might think I cheated, but that doesn't mean that it's true."

"Explain why everyone thinks it, then?"

Leanne took a deep breath. "This is exactly what I never wanted to go back to. I was foolish, I thought it was for the best."

"You thought *what* was for the best? If you slept with Jack while you were with my dad?"

"No, it's not like that!"

"Well, tell me what it was like!"

"It was such a long time ago."

"So? His sister seemed to remember pretty well."

"If she only knew. But then, that was the point…"

"Far out mum, out with it!"

"Ok! Fine! I found out I was pregnant with you, didn't I? I knew Ethan would stick around if he knew and I couldn't do that to him. He had his whole life ahead of him. But he loved me, so how could I make him leave?"

Hannah starred at her mum, unable to comprehend what she was hearing.

"You're unbelievable! You cheated on him to make him *leave*!?"

"But I didn't cheat on him. I only ever made him think I cheated. I never actually went through with it."

Hannah didn't know how to handle this new piece of information. It hurt her to think it was easier for her mum to pretend she cheated, than to tell him the truth, that she was having a baby. Was that news really so terrible?

"So you had everyone think you'd cheated. All because you didn't want anyone to know you were pregnant with me," Hannah looked at her feet.

"Things were different back then. He would have put his career on hold. His parents would have been furious. I would have messed everything up."

"Yeah, and I would have had a dad."

Leanne looked at her daughter. "I'm sorry, Hannah. I had to live with this lie my whole life. Michelle was my best friend, and I never saw her again. She never forgave me. I lost my best friend and my boyfriend because of something I didn't do."

"No, you lost them because of me. If you hadn't been pregnant, you'd still have them. You wouldn't have met Dale, you'd still be…." Hannah had wanted to say 'happy' but the word wouldn't come out. It was too hard for her to take. She had been such a big mistake. She felt unwanted and unloved. She just wanted to get out of her own skin. To be anybody else. Anywhere else.

And now, it was all the more obvious her dad would want nothing to do with her. She had been the reason for so much pain and destruction.

She grabbed her phone and without thinking, she tossed it across the room. It slammed against the coffee table and fell to the floor.

"Keep doing things like that and I'll start to think you're Dale's daughter," said Leanne, unimpressed.

Hannah just glared at her and grabbed her phone. The screen was cracked but it was still working. She headed for her bedroom. Everything about her was pathetic. Her smelly bed, her broken phone, her shabby appearance in the mirror. And now, she didn't even want to speak to Amanda. What was the point? She was just a reminder of everything that could have been, but wasn't. As she thought of Tyler she could feel her anger rise. He didn't even know how good he had it. How could a guy with everything want to lower himself by taking drugs, all to please someone as insignificant as her? *'I guess that's one thing he doesn't have – brains,'* she thought bitterly.

Little feet could be heard at the front of Hannah's bedroom and she looked up to see Chrissie with a concerned look on her face standing in her doorway. "Are you ok?" she asked softly.

"No, I'm not. I'm far from ok," Chrissie looked at her sympathetically. "Is there anything I can do?"

"Not really. Maybe you can change the past. Make sure I'm never born," she said gloomily.

"Why would I want to do that?!"

"You'd all be better off."

"No we wouldn't. I know I wouldn't. You're the one person who makes everything feel better."

Chrissie knelt next to Hannah and grabbed her hand. "Your dad is so going to want to meet you. I know it. Just promise you won't give up."

Hannah patted her sister's head.

"I hope you're right kiddo. I just don't think he'll want anything to do with me."

"Well then he's pretty silly isn't he? Oh well, I guess that means you'll have to stay here with me. It could be worse," she smiled and Hannah's spirits lifted.

"Things would be a whole lot worse if you weren't around," she said. "I'm sorry I've been so focused on finding him, I haven't really been here, focusing on you. And for the record, I wouldn't be going anywhere, even if I did find him. I promise."

"It's ok. I felt silly getting mad at Mrs Carson. I get why you want to find him. I'd like to meet him too."

"Oh really? And why is that?"

She shrugged her shoulders. "Because he's your dad," she said simply.

Hannah smiled and put her arm around her sister. They both had a knack for making each other feel better.

She glanced once again at her phone, grateful that it was still functional. A little reinvigorated, she decided she would call Amanda and fill her in with her mum's side of the story. While she shuddered at the thought of letting her emotion get the better of her, she owed it to Amanda to at least keep her informed. Besides, she would know what to do.

CHAPTER 15

Amanda

Amanda tried to process the latest bombshell as she replayed her latest conversation with Hannah over in her head. Leanne had kept a secret to herself for 15 long years. A secret that had changed everything, in so many ways. Once again, she barely concentrated on her rowdy pupils as she went over the details in her head, and what this new information might mean for Hannah, and for her dad.

Amanda was exhausted by the time she hopped into her car to pick up Jenna and Tyler. She drove absent-mindedly past each traffic light, when her car alerted her to an incoming call. The unexpected noise awoke her from her subconscious and she pulled over to take the call. "Hello?"

"Er, hi. Is this Amanda Carson?"

"Speaking"

"Great. I'm actually returning a call from my sister. She said you were looking to speak to me?"

"Ethan?"

"Yeah, that's right."

"She told you who it was regarding?"

"She mentioned Leanne Thompson. Is she ok?"

"She's fine. It's actually not so much about her. It's about, well, this is hard to explain, particularly over the phone."

"Sorry, I'm not in the country right now, so over the phone is your best bet."

"Right. Well, maybe you should sit down?"

"Look, I haven't seen Leanne in like, forever, it's been ages, so whatever it is…"

"15 years to be exact?"

"Yeah, something like that."

"From the time she cheated on you? Or at least, so you thought."

"Ok. I don't know where you're going with this. But that happened a long time ago. And yeah, I caught her in bed with my best mate, so I'm pretty clear on what happened."

Amanda braced herself. This certainly wasn't how she'd planned on breaking the news. But then, did anything really ever go to plan? She'd just have to come out with it.

"What if I told you that she never went through with it? What if I told you she made you believe she was cheating so that you would break up with her?"

"I'd say that's a nice story, but I know what I saw. Why are you even talking about this, it was a lifetime ago? Who are you?"

"I don't even know where to begin. I called you about this because there's something you should know. And you're finding out 15 years too late. Leanne was pregnant."

Silence.

"Hello?"

"Bullshit."

"No, it's true. You have a daughter and she wants to meet you."

There was more silence.

"Ethan, trust me, I'm not making this up. Why would I? I'm sorry to do this to you, so out of the blue. I told you I didn't want to do this over the phone."

"Can we back up a bit here? You're telling me I have a daughter who must be, what, 15? And she wants to meet me? Sorry but, who *are* you? And how could I have never found out about this? Why now? What's the deal with Leanne? This doesn't make any sense."

"These are all good questions. To be honest, I didn't even know your daughter that long ago. I'm a school teacher. Her sister is in my class. As for Leanne, well… I don't know if I can truly answer that one."

"Why didn't she just tell me? I would have hung around, I would have supported her," he spoke softly now, more to himself than to Amanda.

"Which is exactly why she didn't tell you. She didn't want to burden you, or your family. She said you wanted to make a career and she didn't want to get in the way."

"I would have liked a fucking choice! Sorry. Far out, this is messed up. I don't actually know if I believe you."

"Of course, it's a lot to take in. If you want to know more, maybe we could meet up and we can talk about it? Or you can run away and never look back, pretend this phone call never happened. I wouldn't blame you."

"I could have had a daughter."

"Well, you *do* have a daughter."

"She's 15?"

"Yep. 15. And she wants to meet you. If you want to meet her, obviously."

"This is a lot to get my head around. I think I need some time to process this."

"Of course. Take as long as you need."

"I'm not meant to be back in Sydney until Monday. Where are you based?"

"Melbourne."

"Ok. Far out, just let me think about this. I have to get going. Is this the best number to catch you on?"

"Yeah, this number is best."

"Ok, Bye."

"Bye."

And that was that. Amanda flung the phone down and took a moment herself to process her conversation. The poor guy had not seen it coming. Of course he hadn't. Who expects to return a mysterious phone call from a complete stranger to be told they are the father of a 15 year old girl!? It really was mental. She laughed to herself, wondering what he had expected her to say. Looking back, he had seemed concerned, if anything, for Leanne's wellbeing. Well, that was another story. Maybe he would just have to see for himself. First though, she needed to know if he wanted to meet Hannah. He hadn't said 'no,' so that was a start.

As Amanda arrived home she was greeted by Tyler at the door. "Hey mum, can I stay at Tom's on Friday night?"

"I don't know Tyler, you're still meant to be grounded."

"But I could go there straight after school and then Tom's mum can take us both to the game. Dad won't be home 'til late. He won't know."

"Yes, but I will. Sorry Tyler, it's a no."

"That's so unfair."

"Not really. You're grounded. You're lucky you're even allowed to play football."

"Yeah, only because it would be letting down the team if I didn't play."

"Yes well, you already let Hannah down. No need to let your teammates down as well."

Tyler's expression changed at the mention of Hannah's name. "Do you think she'd want to watch me to play? Do you reckon I can ask her?" Amanda pondered this. "I don't see why not. But you're going to have to wait to ask. I need to make a phone call," the mention of Tom had suddenly given Amanda an idea.

Amanda used to clothes swap with Tom's mum Libby after she'd had Jenna. She'd only stopped in the past year because Libby had gone on a fitness frenzy. She'd lost a heap of weight, meaning they no longer fitted into each other's clothes. Hannah on the other hand, would fit into Libby's clothes perfectly. She marvelled at her brilliant idea, she only hoped Libby would have clothes she was willing to part with. She was probably still bigger than Hannah, but her clothes were designer and would without doubt look better on Hannah than what she was currently stuck with.

She made the phone call and was in luck. Libby had three bags of clothes she was delighted to say were too big for her. Amanda told her she needed them for her niece. It was much easier than explaining the situation with Hannah. Amanda allowed Tyler to go to Tom's place after school on Friday, but she didn't let him stay over. That way, she could pick him up and collect the clothes at the same time.

Tyler received extra good news as he got off the phone to Hannah.

 "She said she would come! I told her you'd pick her up on the way. That way, dad won't know."

"Good thinking."

Amanda was excited at the prospect of Hannah trying on Libby's clothes. They could do it before Tyler's game on Saturday. That way, it wouldn't look like she'd got them specifically for her potential meeting with her dad.

She was a little nervous about how Hannah might respond to being given hand-me-downs, but Amanda thought she could handle it if she went about it the right way. She wanted Ethan to be proud of her daughter, and not to judge her by her appearance. Suddenly Saturday couldn't come soon enough.

CHAPTER 16

Hannah

Hannah was a little suspicious as she, Amanda and Chrissie pulled up outside Amanda's house on Saturday morning. Amanda was acting extremely weird. Hannah couldn't help but wonder if it was something to do with her dad and she was finding it extremely difficult to settle the butterflies in her stomach. They were greeted at the door by Jenna who immediately grabbed Chrissie and dragged her up the stairs.

"Now then," said Amanda a little too enthusiastically. "Hannah, I want to show you something," Hannah looked at her questioningly, her mind wandering. Had she found her dad? Was he here now!?

"Follow me."

She took Hannah upstairs to the spare bedroom. Hannah starred in confusion at the spread of clothing laid out all over the bed.

"I thought you might like to try these!" exclaimed Amanda in excitement.

"I don't get it? You bought me new clothes?"

"Well, no, not exactly. They're my friend's actually. She doesn't fit into them – she's never even worn half of them! She was going to throw them out but she asked me if I knew anyone who might wear them. I thought you might like them?"

Hannah glanced at the clothes, unable to hide the disappointment from her face.

Amanda shared her disappointment, clearly she'd been after a different reaction.

"You don't have to. I just thought you might like them.. I mean, they are really nice.."

"They are. It's just.. you were so excited.. I thought maybe…"

Amanda caught on.

"Oh Hannah, I'm so sorry. I'm such an idiot. I got your hopes up. You thought your dad was here."

"No it's ok, I'm the idiot. As if he would be here," she brushed it off. "Yeah sure, I'll try these on," she could see Amanda's heart literally sink. She hadn't meant to make her feel bad. She tried to get excited about the clothes on the bed.

"I thought you could have a bit of fun with it. I got my makeup and GHD ready in the ensuite. I thought you could get all dressed up. It sounded a lot more fun in my head, now it just seems silly. I'm sorry." She spoke fast and was acting all embarrassed. Hannah wished she hadn't gotten herself worked up. She looked closely at the jackets and jeans on the bedspread. She'd never even heard of half of the brands. Part of her wanted to yell at Amanda for being so thoughtless. Shouldn't she have known she'd have been thinking about her dad after she'd been acting so happy? But then, she could see how bad she felt and grabbed the closest jeans and jumper. She took a beige colour coat with her too. She had to do a double-take. Was this cashmere? Amanda left her to get changed. She put on the outfit and looked in the mirror. The clothes felt amazing and they looked great, she just felt completely out of place as she looked back at herself in the mirror. What was that saying she had heard of? Mutton dressed as lamb? She felt like a donkey dressed as a unicorn. You could wear the horn, but who were you really fooling? She took off the coat and picked up the makeup bag. Maybe she'd feel better with a bit of foundation. She found herself enjoying putting on the makeup. She added a bit of bronzer and a touch of blush. She was actually good at applying makeup, despite how little she used it. But then, she'd had a bit of practice touching up her bruises. Hannah dismissed that thought and searched for some mascara.

Once she had finished with her face she re-checked herself in the mirror. Perhaps now the unicorn was a little more convincing. She smiled at herself and turned on the GHD. She didn't want to admit it to herself, but she was having fun. And she looked good. Really good. There was just something off about it as she ran the GHD through her hair. She felt awkward, like she was looking at someone else in the mirror. But then, hadn't she wanted to be someone else?

She put the coat back on and did up the buttons. She found a pair of knee-high boots amongst a pile of shoes on the floor. She never would have contemplated trying anything like them, but heck, if the boot fits! She zipped them up and looked at herself side on. She looked 5 years older! The transformation was crazy. Could she really pull this off? She wasn't convinced.

She opened the bedroom door and stepped out. Amanda gasped.

"Wow! Hannah! What do you think!?"

"I don't know. I feel fake," Hannah shrugged. She couldn't deny it. She didn't feel right. She was confused with how she was felt. This should have been everything she wanted, yet instead it felt off.

"What do you mean?"

"I don't know. Like this isn't me. I feel weird."

Amanda gave her a disapproving look.

"Hannah, you don't have to be what everyone else perceives you to be. You can be whoever you want. I think you look great."

"Really?" she asked, unsure.

"Absolutely! Now come on! I can't wait to see Tyler's face when he sees you!"

Hannah smiled weakly. She checked herself in the mirror once more. She really didn't look like herself, or feel like herself. But then, maybe that was the best part. Besides, part of her couldn't wait to see Tyler's face either. She followed Amanda and the girls to the car and hopped in, the butterflies returning full of flutter to her stomach.

Amanda

Amanda couldn't believe the transformation. She'd had to blink back the tears as Hannah had stood in front of her. She looked incredible. She had so much to offer, and not just on the outside, which Amanda was seeing now. She was caring and smart and completely oblivious to the potential within her. She had never had anyone to tell her how special she was, no one to allow her to believe it. That was the hardest part. Because who knew what she could be if she'd had a different upbringing. Was there enough time to change the way she saw herself? Or had the damage already been done? As Amanda looked at the girl in front of her, she saw so many possibilities. Despite the makeover, Hannah still struggled to see it. It was like she couldn't believe what she saw in the mirror, *wouldn't* believe that the image reflecting back at her, was her.

Amanda wanted to shake her, to tell her that she was everything she saw in the mirror, and so much more. She had no doubt now that Ethan would see it. How could you not? The only thing holding her back was her own doubt. She wondered if her dad could be the very person to change that.

She could only hope he would give her the chance.

*

The girls chatted away in the back of the car while Amanda did her best not to keep glancing across at Hannah. She literally couldn't believe her eyes. She really couldn't wait for Tyler's reaction, or even Danny's. Would he see her any differently?

They pulled up at the ground and Jenna asked if they could play on the playground. Amanda walked Jenna and Chrissie to the swings with Hannah following close behind. Amanda couldn't help but notice a group of teenage boys glance at Hannah, looking her up and down. Amanda smiled to herself; she was a genius.

Amanda could tell that Hannah didn't really know what to do with herself. "You don't have to stand with me Hannah, I don't mind."

Hannah peered across at her sister. "I might go push Chrissie for a bit. I'll come back when the game starts." "No worries," replied Amanda. She looked at her watch. She wondered how long it would take for one of the guys to approach her. She was momentarily distracted as the Tigers came out for their warm up. They did a few drills before a stray ball was kicked against the fence. Tyler headed over to pick it up.

"Didn't Hannah end up coming?" he asked as he leant down to pick up the ball. "Yeah, she did. She's just at the swings with the girls," Amanda pointed across at the playground, and sure enough, a sandy haired boy stood next to her, chatting in her ear. "Where?" asked Tyler. "*There,*" Amanda pointed again, enjoying the look of surprise as Tyler finally realised the girl pushing Chrissie was indeed Hannah. He didn't say anything for a few seconds. He received a ball to the back of the head "Oi! Ty! What are you doing! Keep moving!" He turned back around to join his teammates. Amanda heard one of them ask who the girl was. She chuckled to herself as she heard Tyler respond by asking if any of them knew who the guy talking to her was.

'Let this be a much needed confidence boost,' she thought.

Amanda stood bemused as Hannah returned. "Who was your friend?" she asked innocently. Hannah shrugged. "I dunno. Some guy. What number is Tyler?" she asked as the players now stood in their positions, ready for the ball to bounce. "He's number 7. You missed him earlier, before the game. He didn't even recognise you. Mind you, I think he was more concerned about the guy you were speaking to."

"Oh, did he know him?" asked Hannah, completely oblivious. "No, but I think he wanted to. He was green with envy," Hannah shifted her feet uncomfortably. "I wonder if he'd be like that if I wasn't dressed like… this," Amanda raised her eyebrows. "Give yourself some credit. Ty's been into you since way before your makeover, we both know that."

Hannah didn't say anything. Amanda had a feeling she knew what Hannah was thinking. He had gone about showing his feelings in the complete wrong way. She wasn't sure if she'd forgiven him entirely, but then, she'd come to watch him play so that had to mean something. "I don't get it," said Hannah suddenly. "Get what?"

"I dunno, you almost seem to want me and Tyler to get together, or something. I just, I wouldn't have thought you'd think I was his type."

Amanda smiled. "Hannah, you might not think too highly of yourself, but I've been with you from the start. My *perfect* son could do a lot worse. I wish I could make you see that."
"You hardly even know me."
"What is there to know? You're stubborn, blunt and really hard to read sometimes. You're also funny, albeit a little sarcastic, thoughtful and empathetic. Tyler likes you, and I like stirring him up. Maybe I like stirring you up, too. Besides, don't you like him?" She winked, wondering how much she could get away with. Hannah glared at her, but not in an aggressive way. She almost smiled. Before she could say anything, Amanda's phone buzzed. She didn't recognise the number, so she thought she could take a guess who it might be. Not wanting to answer the call in front of Hannah, she asked her to keep an eye on Chrissie and Jenna while she took the call.

"Hi, Amanda?"
"Yes?"

"It's me again, Ethan. Look, I've had a think about our conversation and I'm not going to be able to concentrate on anything else. I've had a look at flights and I can make it in to Melbourne next Saturday. What are the chances of us meeting then?"

Amanda had to take a moment to process this information. He was going to come to Melbourne next weekend!

"Um, yes, sure ok, let's do that. Now when you say 'us'…"

"I think I want to meet her. But Jesus, you have to understand how unreal this is to me. I don't even know who you are. You're just some stranger who's turned my life upside down. But if what you're saying is true, then yeah, I want to meet her. I need to meet you first, though. I just can't get my head around this and I don't know if I believe you. Leanne cheated on me and she left. Now you're telling me a different story. It all happened so long ago, you have to understand how hard this is for me to take." He took a breath.

"Of course. It's a crazy story, and I guess a lot has changed in 15 years. Your daughter doesn't know I've managed to track you down, but now that you potentially *do* want to meet her, I could probably fill her in. But it would be best if I meet you first. You're right, you don't know me, and we don't know you. Just give me some time to figure all this out. I wasn't really expecting this to happen so soon."

Amanda may not 'know' Ethan, but Danny had run a background check at least. She definitely needed to see for herself though and meet face to face.

"I can wait. If I have to, I guess. I can't believe this is happening."

"No, no, the sooner the better. If you're ok to change your plans?"

"Yeah, it's no drama. This conference has been a waste of time anyway."

"Ok, well, what do you say we meet on Saturday? If you decide it's something you still want to go ahead with, maybe we could arrange for you to meet Hannah on Sunday? Are you in Melbourne all weekend?"

"Hannah. Shit I didn't even ask her name! Um, yeah ok. I can be in Melbourne for the weekend. Let me just sort out my arrangements and we'll organise somewhere to meet?"

"Sounds great. Well I better go, speak soon Ethan."

"Ok, bye.

She hung up the phone and felt the butterflies dance in her stomach. She was going to meet Hannah's dad, and then Hannah would most likely meet him too! She couldn't believe it. He sounded ok over the phone. Heck, he had to be better than Dale. And he sounded keen to meet Hannah! That could only be a good thing too.

She couldn't decide if she should tell Hannah or not. What if they met on Saturday and she got a bad vibe? What if he changed his mind?

She glanced across at Hannah, who was unaware of the fact that she'd just been speaking to her dad. Should she tell her the news, or should she wait? Her mind raced as she thought out each scenario. The longer she lingered, the more suspicious Hannah would become.

She decided not to tell her. Not just yet. She didn't want to get her hopes up and a week was a long time for Ethan to change his mind.

They continued to watch Tyler as Amanda tried to act normal. She felt like Hannah kept watching her, like she anticipated she was about to share some exciting news.

"So, what do you think? Was it worth coming to watch?" Amanda asked as the final siren sounded. Hannah shrugged. "Yeah, I guess. I don't really get the game, but he got a lot of the ball."

"He didn't play that well. He didn't even kick a goal!" pipped up Jenna.

The four of them made their way to the change rooms, Hannah

like usual didn't say anything else. They entered the rooms and spotted Tyler. They made their way over and he smiled, a little more shy than normal. "Thanks for coming. Only, I could have played better." "I know right, you didn't even kick a goal," said Hannah, cheekily. Amanda wanted to leave them alone, but she couldn't help herself. "So, what do you think Ty? Like Hannah's new look?" She had probably over stepped it. Hannah was back to looking at her with devil eyes, and Tyler was clearly embarrassed. "Sure, you look... different," he said, looking Hannah up and down. Different!? He had gone with *different!?* 'Oh Tyler'. Hannah raised her eyebrows. "Different? What's that supposed to mean?" "I dunno... like, yeah, you look different."

 He was lost for words and Hannah was taking it the complete wrong way. Couldn't she see he was speechless because she'd taken his breath away? *'Boys,'* she thought, rolling her eyes. "So anyway, did you want to maybe grab a bite to eat? The canteen is still open... we could go for a walk?"

"No, actually I better be getting back home. I'll see you later," and just like that, she turned around and left. Tyler looked completely put out, and if anything else, shocked. "Did I do something?" he asked. "My God, Ty. "*Different*!" That's what you come out with!?" "What? She does look different." Amanda rolled her eyes once more and followed Hannah outside.

"Hey!" she shouted after her. "Are you ok?" Hannah didn't say anything. She seemed to hate sharing her thoughts. Amanda didn't know what to say. She had been relying on Tyler for the self-esteem boost. She could tell Hannah felt uncomfortable, and possibly even hurt. "I think I should go home," Hannah said the words but Amanda didn't really think she meant them. "Really? You want to go home?" Hannah shrugged. "No but I, I just want to be alone."

 Amanda couldn't read Hannah. She seemed confused and if anything, lost. She didn't know whether to comfort her or if she really did want to be alone. She attempted to reassure her. "Tyler was just being daft. He clearly thought you looked great, you had him speechless!"

"I don't care. It's not that. I don't know. I just, can we go?"

"Ok, you really want me to take you home?" Hannah nodded but Amanda wasn't convinced. "Ok, well if you're sure. I'll just go get Chrissie. Danny can take Jenna," Hannah nodded.

Amanda tried in vain to make conversation with Hannah as they headed back to her house. She couldn't understand why she was acting so strangely. Surely Tyler's comment wasn't the reason? It seemed like an extreme reaction. She also couldn't decide whether to tell her about her dad. It was certainly an opportunity to brighten her mood. But then, she couldn't afford the other side if he let her down. She bit her tongue. As they pulled up, she took satisfaction in the fact that there was still no sign of Dale's car. She opened the car boot and pulled out an additional bag of clothes. She handed it to Hannah. "Here, there's some more stuff in there for you to try. Or you can put them straight in the bin, I don't mind."

Hannah took the clothes but didn't say anything. She headed for the door, ushering Chrissie inside.

"See you tomorrow Chrissie, and Hannah, call me if you need me," she yelled, but they were already inside.

Hannah

Chrissie headed straight to the toilet as Hannah shut the front door. She leant against it, feeling more flat than she had in a long time. She couldn't exactly pinpoint what had triggered it. Surely it couldn't be what she thought it was? Because while Tyler hadn't exactly said what she thought, or indeed hoped he would say, that surely couldn't be the cause of the shattered feeling she now felt.

She had longed for him to look at her in awe, in admiration. She had wanted to feel something different. She hadn't wanted to be told she *looked* different. He certainly hadn't looked at her in the way the other guys had looked at her at the playground. In fact, if anything he had looked disappointed. She felt let down. She felt phony. She felt like all her doubts about herself had been confirmed. Who had she been fooling? Tyler had seen straight through her. Seen her for what she really was. That trashy rat he'd always seen her as. Her negative thoughts began to consume her and she headed for her bedroom, brushing away the tears as she closed her bedroom door.

She rubbed her eyes and looked in the mirror. That probably wasn't a great idea. The mascara smudged around her eyes, making her look even more average than ever. She swung the pile of clothes onto her bed and leant against her bedside table. She ran her hands through her hair in frustration. She was sick and tired of her constant tears, her constant emotions. Couldn't she just for one minute not cry over every little thing? Why did she have to be so pathetic, and why did she think her dad would even consider meeting her? And so what if he did? He would just be disappointed.

But then, a familiar voice popped into her head. 'He was into you before the makeover.' Maybe Amanda had a point. Tyler had been trying to impress her before her fancy clothes. And shouldn't that be more important? He had liked her for her. He hadn't needed the heavy makeup or the designer outfit. Sure, she might have always wanted to be someone else. But above all, she wanted someone to *see* her as someone else. Tyler had done that, she just hadn't realised it. Maybe that was why she had felt so strange. These clothes, this style, it wasn't her. She didn't feel right in them because they weren't her. Maybe she *would* be ok in her own skin. Tyler seemed to think she was ok.

She picked herself up off the floor and undid the garbage bag of clothes. As she got out the clothes she found a few that were a little more casual. Clothes she could still be herself in. Feeling better about herself, she separated the clothes into categories: "keep," "no chance" and "maybe someday." Satisfied, she put her "keep" clothes in her top drawer, her "maybe someday" clothes in the bottom drawer and placed the rest back into the garbage bag. She had to hand it to Amanda. She wasn't even here and yet she'd managed to make her smile. She wondered how she'd gotten by so long without her. She smiled again to herself. She definitely wouldn't be telling Amanda that.

CHAPTER 17

Amanda

It took a whole 24 hours before Amanda decided it was time to break the exciting news to Hannah. She knew it was risky, but she'd had good vibes from Ethan and it was just the news she needed to lift Hannah's spirits. The only issue was, she didn't want Leanne to find out that she had spoken to Ethan. While she could word up Hannah not to say anything, Leanne might still get suspicious that Amanda had made the call. Or, she could be completely off her head and not even realise. That thought didn't help, instead it made her sick to think she had left Hannah and Chrissie in her hands. She still wasn't convinced that had been a wise move, even if it had proved to be ok so far. Still, Dale could return home at any moment and then who knew what would happen?

She shuddered to herself but was momentarily distracted as Jenna jumped up and down, clinging to her arm. "What's for dinner, mummy? Mummy, can you make bangers and mash? Please mummy?"

"Go ask your brother if he'll start up the Barbie?" she replied in the hopes of getting her daughter off her arm.

 She scrummaged through the fridge and cupboard to see what ingredients she had. If Tyler operated the BBQ, dinner would be nice and simple. Amanda got out some potatoes and butter to prepare her mash potatoes. As she was preparing her salad, she dialled Hannah's number.

"Hello?"

"Hi, Hannah. Sorry to be the one calling you but, I've got some news. Really *good* news this time. Is anyone else around right now?"

"No. Well, mum and my sister are home, but they aren't around. Dale's still not back."

"Ok. It's just, I need to speak to you discretely. Just don't mention what I'm about to say around your mum ok – she's definitely not there?"

"No, I don't know where she is."

"Ok. Well, the good news is I spoke to your dad! Everything's all happening so quickly. I don't want to get your hopes up, but there's a chance you might meet him this weekend. I just don't want you to tell your mum. She might get involved and mess things up. He sounds pretty keen, Hannah but I'm going to meet with him first…Hannah, are you there?"

"Aha… I just… don't know what to say… he still wants to meet me?"

"That's what he said. But we thought it would be a good idea if I met with him first. I need to suss him out a bit, then I'll get the all clear."

"Ok."

"So, I don't know how we're going to work this but the plan if all goes well is for you two to meet next Sunday. Will you be home?"

"Yeah."

"Great, well if all goes well, I'll pick you up from yours at 11am on Sunday and we'll go from there. Just be discrete, OK? I don't want to mess this up."

"Ok."

"If anything changes I'll call you. It'd be good if your mum was out of the house. I really don't want her to know we've found him so soon. I know she's going to want to meet him too and I'd

prefer not. Not yet."
"Ok."
"So I'll see you at 11am on Sunday, if everything goes well."
"Ok."

Hannah

Hannah hung up the phone and her mind raced. Amanda had spoken to her dad. She had found him. She couldn't comprehend this realisation. Her mind simply wouldn't process that it was real. Could she actually be about to meet him? As soon as Sunday!? It all felt so surreal, like it couldn't actually be true. She tried not to get her hopes up, but it was hard not to. She didn't know how to act, how to think, how to feel. She had never had good news like this before. She sat in a haze, starring at the wall when her mum and sister appeared from the bathroom.
"It will stop bleeding if you just put pressure on it."
"But it hurts," whined Chrissie. Hannah didn't even blink. She just sat in a daze staring at the kitchen bench.
"And what's wrong with you?"
"What? Nothing."
"Good. Would you mind helping Chrissie, then? She's given herself a paper cut and it won't stop bleeding."
Hannah didn't move.
"Hannah? Did you hear what I said?"
"Huh?"
"Your sister. For God's sakes I asked you to help her."
"Right. What's up?"
Chrissie shook her head. "Never mind, I think it stopped."
"Cool," replied Hannah absent-mindedly and she headed for her bedroom.
Chrissie followed her sister with tissue in hand.
"Did something happen? You look shocked."

Hannah looked down at her sister, contemplating whether to tell her. She had to share her news with someone, and who better than Chrissie?

"Can you keep a secret?" she asked

"Yes."

"Do you promise?"

"I promise."

"Cross you heart?"

"Yes!"

"You especially can't tell mum, ok?"

"Ok. What is it?"

"I'm going to meet my dad."

"What!? When?"

"On Sunday. I hope. But you have to keep it quiet. I don't want mum to know."

"Ok."

"I might need you to do me a favour, too. Do you reckon you could convince mum to take you out? Even just for a walk or something? I don't want her to have any idea. She could spoil everything."

Chrissie looked put out.

"Does that mean I won't get to meet him either?"

"Sure you can. Just not on Sunday. Do you think you could do that? For me?"

"Ok. But I really do want to meet him too. Promise you'll let me?"

"Deal."

They wrapped their pinkie fingers around one another.

"Are you excited?"

"I don't know. It hasn't really sunk in. Mrs Carson is going to meet with him first. She'll probably tell him to run away fast."

"Why would she do that?" asked Chrissie.

"I don't know. I just feel like this isn't real. I never thought I'd actually find him."

"I wonder when my daddy is going to come home. I miss him still…even though…" she trailed off and tried to blink back her tears.

"It's ok Chrissie, he's your dad. You're allowed to miss him."

"Even if he scares me? I've never seen him…like that before."

Hannah was taken back to that moment when Dale had stood over her with the whisky bottle and her sister had appeared, petrified in the doorway. It was not something she wanted to relive.

Maybe, just maybe, she would never have to. She wondered what Ethan, what her dad, was like. Hopefully he would never want to harm her or abuse her, or take advantage of her with his friends. Hannah was brought back to that moment in her bedroom when she had felt violated. She still wasn't entirely sure what happened or how far they'd gone. She'd just wanted to forget about it. Besides, how was she meant to know? She was never going to confront him about it. She never wanted to relive that moment, let alone give him the satisfaction. If only she could seek revenge and make him pay for the years of pain and torment. Maybe the biggest revenge of all was walking away and never letting him hurt her again. Could her dad provide her with that outlet? The prospect of that turning into a reality seemed all the more closer now, but she wouldn't allow herself to get her hopes up. After all, what if she didn't even like him? What if he didn't like her? That scenario seemed all the more probable. She couldn't think of a reason why she wouldn't like her biological father. He was her real father, and he had to be an improvement on Dale.

Yet the chances of him accepting her were slim. He had his own life to get on with. Who was she, other than some mistake he'd never even known existed until 5 minutes ago? And she was 15. Surely he would see that as a negative. Her adverse thoughts consumed her and she became more and more uneasy. Suddenly Sunday couldn't come quick enough. At least then she would know. She'd be able to see it in his eyes.

CHAPTER 18

Hannah

Hannah paced around the kitchen table impatiently on Sunday morning as she waited for Chrissie and Leanne to depart. Chrissie had managed to convince her mum to take her for a walk. She was going to take her to the café so she could try another muffin. The very same café Hannah was meant to have her interview. Of course, Leanne had wanted Hannah to take her, but Hannah had promised to clean the kitchen instead. It was a promise she would be breaking, but she wasn't too worried about the consequence. For one, it was Dale who dished out the harsh punishments and two, what she was about to do would be worth whatever punishment her mum gave her. Hannah had decided to leave Chrissie with her phone. Hannah wouldn't be needing it and it gave her peace of mind leaving her sister alone with her mum.

The two of them both finally left the house and Chrissie gave her sister a secret thumbs up as she walked out the door.

As the door closed Hannah reached into her pocket and pulled out the photo of her dad she had been carrying with her ever since she had discovered his existence. She starred at it longingly, knowing she was only hours away from meeting him face to face. As the time drew closer to 11 o'clock, Hannah made a final stop at the bathroom to ease her nerves. She washed her hands and looked at her reflection in the mirror. She hoped her dad wouldn't be too disappointed with what he saw. She was skinny and scrawny, but hopefully he would recognise her pale blue eyes.

The beep of the horn outside distracted her, she brushed her fingers through her hair and raced out the door. She was too full of emotion to realise she'd left the photo of her dad on the kitchen table.

Amanda

Amanda couldn't have been happier with how things had gone with Ethan, and she relived yesterday's events as she made her way to collect Hannah.

Amanda had arranged to meet in the lobby of Ethan's hotel, and he was already there waiting when she arrived. She had no trouble spotting him. He really didn't look that much different from the 15 year old photos she had seen. He was well dressed in a white shirt and slim fitting jeans. As she approached him and said hello he got out of his chair and shook her hand. "Hi, Amanda? Nice to put a face to a voice," he said and smiled politely. His eyes were the same pale shade of blue as Hannah's. "I feel like I already know you, I've seen lots of photos and you look just the same. Nice to meet you."

She sat down and any awkwardness she had anticipated disappeared in an instant.

"Yeah, nice to meet you too."

"I'm sorry to catch you off guard with all of this. I know it's a lot to process."

Ethan raised his eyebrows. "You can say that agai," but he said it with a smile and it reassured her.

"So, anything in particular you want to know? I haven't killed anybody or been to jail. I've had a couple of speeding fines, that's about it."

Amanda laughed.

"Actually, maybe we can start a little smaller. Your sister mentioned you were a chiropractor, how long have you been doing that?"

"Yeah, that's what I'm qualified as. I've taken a step back a little bit now and set up my own clinic in Sydney. These days I mainly run the clinic and attend the odd conference, and I still see a few long term clients here and there."

"Cool, so you live in Sydney?"

"Surry Hills."

"Nice. I'm sorry, this is so weird. I feel like I'm at a job interview but I want to ask you personal questions… do you have a family?"

"Actually, I don't. I've had the odd girlfriend here and there but my career has always been my priority. Maybe Leanne did have a point. I'm sure things could have been different, if she'd let me. I've just never really met anyone worth settling down for. I'm actually seeing someone casually now, but it's very early days, who knows – maybe she's the one," he joked nervously and Amanda felt a little uncomfortable. It was weird to have someone she didn't know tell her their life story.

"But enough of me. What's Hannah like? She must be what, Year 10?"

Amanda was happy he was keen to talk about Hannah.

"Hannah is…gosh how do I sum her up? You're going to need to give her some time. She hasn't had the easiest upbringing. She's quiet and distant, yet she's funny and intuitive. She definitely has trust issues, so you're going to have to build on that, I mean, depending on how tomorrow goes I guess. One step at a time"

Ethan nodded, taking in the information.

"What do you mean she hasn't had the easiest upbringing? I would have thought Leanne would have been right with that?"

Amanda sighed.

"That's another story. Things happen, people change. I'm sure she was a good mum at one stage, but she met this guy and well, things went a bit pear shaped."

"Is she married?"

"No."

"But she lives with him?"
"Yeah, they have another daughter together."
"I see."
The two of them sat in awkward silence for a moment, before he laughed out loud to himself.
"It's funny, the things you remember. She used to be a great cook, and she used to love to take the piss. She had a great sense of humour." He drifted off and starred into the distance, reminiscing about a different time. "I guess that's what I remember most. Then she did what she did and I never saw her again. That's when I focused even harder on my career and opened my own clinic. Great clinic, shitty name," he smiled to himself.
Amanda smiled. "It's 'Even Stevens' right?"
He raised his eyebrows, surprised. "Yeah, it is. How did you know?"
"I rang your office. I found your office before I found your sister. But you were at your conference. My husband is a lawyer, that's how we managed to find you. Look, I know you want to meet Hannah, but I have to warn you about Leanne. She's not the same girl you knew all those years ago."
Ethan nodded.
"I never forgave her for what she did. And now I find out she lied about it. I don't know what's worse. I'd never wish anything bad on her, though and I hope she's ok. But right now, I just want to meet Hannah. I just want to meet my daughter."
He looked her in the eyes and she couldn't help but trust him.
"She's just used to being let down. I guess I just wanted to make sure you weren't keen on meeting Hannah just so you can reconnect with her mum."
Ethan shook his head.
"I'm not going to lie, it saddens me to hear Leanne's not in a good place. But it's not about her. I haven't thought about her in years. And then out of nowhere I find out I'm a dad. I just wish I'd known sooner. 15 years is a lot of wasted time."
"Well, that's something you and Hannah will definitely agree on. She's thought about you her whole life, she's just never seen

the point in trying to find you."

"And now, here we are."

They continued to chat for another hour. Ethan told her about his sister, his business and how he'd never even ended up going overseas. He'd ended up moving to Sydney and staying with his uncle.

Amanda couldn't help but feel upset at the lost opportunity. One stupid little lie had changed their paths completely. At least Ethan's had turned out for the best. He seemed happy, healthy and content, and she could tell he was getting more and more excited at the prospect of meeting his daughter. She just hoped she had prepared him enough. Hannah wasn't exactly like most kids. There were parts of her that were so much more. She so hoped he would see that. He would just need time.

Amanda was brought back to the present as she pulled up outside Hannah's house. She beeped the horn. It was the safer move in case Leanne was still home. She was just about to beep again when the door opened and Hannah raced out to the car.

Amanda couldn't help but feel a touch of disappointment as Hannah stepped out. She had been hoping she would be all dressed up, given that she'd left her with a whole bag of outfits to choose from. Instead, she wore a pair of casual jeans, a black Nike jumper and the same Dunlop shoes she always wore.

She opened the door and hopped in.

"Hey."

"Hi," Amanda said, having difficulty hiding the disappointment from her face.

"What?" Hannah asked, looking down at herself.

"Nothing, it's just, well, I don't mean this in the wrong way but I thought you would have dressed up today. Meeting your dad for the first time, you know…" she cringed at herself. She sounded like such a snob.

"I thought about it. But then I figured, what's the point? I mean, those clothes are nice, but they aren't really me. This is about meeting my dad, and my dad meeting me. If he's going to accept me, it's going to be because he accepts me for me. If he doesn't, if he thinks I'm something I'm not, then what's the point of all this?"

Amanda smiled and suppressed a laugh.

"You surprise me sometimes, you know," she said. Amanda was taken aback. All this time, she thought she'd been the one helping Hannah, yet maybe it was Hannah who was helping her. She was enabling her to see things from a different perspective.

"I don't know why. You're the one who told me Tyler liked me before. Why should this be any different? There's no point pretending to be something I'm not. I'm telling you what you already know."

"Yes, I guess you are," replied Amanda, shocked at the wise words from the small town girl who said so little.

"Well, this is it."

Hannah nodded.

"How are you feeling?"

Hannah shrugged.

"Excited? Nervous? Sick?"

"Yep."

"Don't worry. He's so excited to meet you."

"I hope he's not disappointed."

"Don't be stupid."

They didn't say anything to each other for the next 10 minutes. Hannah just sat starring out the window as usual until she jumped unexpectedly.

"Crap."

"What is it?"

"I left the photo of dad on the kitchen table. Mum's going to find it."

"Do you want me to go back?"

"No, don't worry about it. I forgot to write her a note to say I'd gone out. She'll probably figure out what I'm doing now. Oh well."

"Well, at least she doesn't know where you're meeting. It probably won't matter if she finds out now anyway. I just didn't want her to know before today. She might have tried to sabotage it." Hannah still looked worried.

"Honestly, don't worry about it. Just think about meeting your dad. We're not too far away now. He was seriously excited to meet you."

"Did you find out anything else about him?"

"Let's see. He lives in Surry Hills. He has his own Chiropractic clinic. It's called 'Even Stevens'. It's in Sydney. He doesn't have a family, he's been pretty focused on his career…"

"Wait, did you say his clinic is called 'Even Stevens'?" "Yeah, he said it was a shitty name, but I thought it was kind of clever." "That's weird."

"What, that he called it something he doesn't like?"

"No, 'Even Stevens'. That's what mum used to call him." Hannah looked puzzled. Amanda pondered this new information.

"I don't know, Hannah. He said he hadn't thought about your mum in 15 years; that he never forgave her. But I think there's a part of him that never really let go." "Imagine if he'd stayed. Mum could have been so happy. I could have been happy."

"Well, maybe try and look at the positives. Maybe if he did stay, you'd never have had a sister. You'd never have had Chrissie."

Hannah thought about this. "That's true, I guess. Chrissie actually ended up being pretty good about all this. She's been pretty good about everything really, considering everything she's seen…" Hannah tapered off and bit her tongue, as though she'd said too much. Amanda wasn't having it though.

"What do you mean?"

"Nothing.."

"Really?"

Hannah looked as though she was contemplating whether to say more. Amanda decided to let it play out.

"It's just…"

Amanda kept driving. Was Hannah finally opening up to her?

"If someone… if you did it…"

"Did what?"

"You know…it."

"Mm..."

"Well, let's say you were out of it when it happened. And you woke up the next day. Would you know if you'd done it?"

"As in, you were high and passed out and can't remember if you did it?"

"Not exactly. Can we just pretend, or say, hypothetically, I was talking about a friend... and she was unconscious... and she thought maybe someone took advantage... is there any way for her to know for sure. What would her symptoms be?"

Amanda tried to concentrate on driving while comprehending the information she was receiving.

Hannah had barely strung more than a sentence together the whole time she'd known her, unless she was speaking about her dad. Now, she was asking a highly confronting and downright concerning question right before her most anticipated moment.

"Hannah. Are you trying to tell me that you, or let's say your 'friend', that you think she was raped?"

Hannah remained silent.

Amanda tried to concentrate on her driving and answer Hannah's questions. "There would be a couple of symptoms, like pain, especially in t*hat* region, bruising, blood on the sheets, undies; those are some of them. Does that help?"

Hannah nodded.

"Hannah, this is really serious. I hope you don't mean what I think you mean. This needs to be reported to the police, straight away."

"It didn't happen recently. Not super recently. Nobody told the police. Can we just drop it now? I don't know why I brought it up."

"Because you need to speak about it. Far out, no one should have to go through that alone. I don't even know what to say. I'm sorry.

"It's not your fault."

No, but bloody hell. Let's just go meet your dad, huh." She really didn't know what to say. It was too much for her to bear. Had

Hannah's step dad really gone that far? No matter how much Hannah wanted no interference, Amanda really should have phoned the police. Or notified Jenny. Or told someone!

They finally pulled up outside the hotel and Amanda's phone buzzed. She had received a text message from Hannah's phone. She must have left it with Chrissie. Smart thinking.

She opened the message and her heart sank. The coded message she had given to Hannah in case of an emergency read across her screen. "23 yellow flowers" Given that Hannah was getting out of the car alongside her, they could only have come from one other person.

Chrissie was in trouble and Amanda couldn't believe the timing. Had Dale returned home? Amanda didn't have the heart to tell Hannah, not right now. But she needed to act fast. She tried to remain calm.

"Sorry, Hannah, I've got to make a really quick phone call. Would you mind waiting in the car? I'll only be a sec."

She keyed in 000 and requested the police. She reported an anonymous disturbance at Hannah's address. She hung up the phone and tried to ignore the sick feeling in her stomach.

She smiled at Hannah as she opened the driver door. "Are you ready?"

"I think so," she said and hopped out of the car. Amanda looked at her watch. "We've made pretty good time. Do you want to grab a bite to eat while we wait? He probably won't be here for another half hour or so."

"I don't think I can eat. Maybe just a lemonade?"

"Good idea." Amanda didn't think she could eat right now either.

They sat in silence as the minutes ticked over. Amanda felt unbearably sick and she couldn't handle not knowing what was going on back at Hannah's house. Was Chrissie ok? Should she be trying to phone her? What if she was hiding somewhere and her ringing phone brought attention to her? She felt so hopeless and upset, only made worse by keeping Chrissie's text secret from Hannah. It was the last thing she needed right now, right before she was finally about to meet her dad. Amanda simply couldn't spoil this moment. There was nothing Hannah could do for her sister right now anyway. Amanda glanced at her watch when her phone rang. It was Jenny. "I'm sorry Hannah, I've really got to get this."

She got up out of her seat before Hannah could respond. "Hi Jenny."

"Mandy, I'm really sorry to bother you on the weekend but this is quite important. I have just been notified of a disturbance at Christina Thompson's house. The police were called. Chrissie is ok but she's been taken by child services. Her mother has been taken to hospital, she's been badly beaten. Her boyfriend is in custody. That's all I know at this stage. As soon as I know more I'll let you know. Don't expect Chrissie to be at school tomorrow and probably longer."

"Holy crap. That's horrible. Is Leanne ok?"

"She was rushed to hospital in an ambulance, I don't know much else, I'm sorry. I'll meet with you tomorrow morning. I just wanted to let you know."

"Ok, thanks."

She hung up the phone and felt helplessly bad. She looked across at Hannah. She just couldn't bring herself to tell her what had happened. She couldn't do that to her, not now. It would have to wait. Guilt swept over her as she tried to comprehend the news Jenny had given her. Dale had obviously returned home, but what had caused him to behave like that?

She couldn't help but feel responsible. She should have followed her head and not her heart. She should have told someone what she knew, before it was too late. And maybe now it was. How could she have been so reckless? All to obey a teenager she barely even knew. Hannah would surely think differently too if she knew what Amanda had just found out. She had stayed silent to protect Chrissie, but what good had that done?

She sat back down next to Hannah and tried to act normal. Hannah seemed too caught up in her own nerves to notice anything different.

Suddenly, she stood up.

"That's him," she whispered. Amanda turned around, and there he was, smiling broadly.

He came towards the table.

"Hi Amanda, nice to see you again. And you must be Hannah, he looked down at her warmly and Hannah was overwhelmed. She couldn't speak. "Hi," she said, faintly.

"Well!" said Amanda. "I guess I'll leave the two of you to it. I think you have a bit to catch up on."

"Yeah, just 15 years or so," said Ethan with a laugh as he glanced at Hannah. "Well, it was lovely seeing you again Ethan. I'll be back in a couple of hours, but I'm not too far away. I'll see you both soon."

She looked at Hannah and again had an awkward feeling of not knowing how to approach her to say goodbye. Before she could move, Hannah wrapped her arms around her, hugging her tight. She let go quickly and wiped her eyes.

"Thanks. For everything. You've been… well, thanks," Hannah's emotion got the better of her and she hid her face in her hands. "Sorry. Dammit, I promised myself I wouldn't cry."

Amanda smiled. "Well that was silly of you. You of all people should know not to make promises you don't know if you can keep."

Hannah looked at her, and a grin spread across her face. Boy, what a difference it made. "You kept yours. You did it. I honestly don't know what to say."

"Well, that's nothing new. Now go meet your dad," It was Amanda's turn to wipe her eyes. She felt so pleased for Hannah, yet the happiness had a hollowness for fear of what was to come. How was she going to break it to her that her mum was in hospital and her sister had been taken away?

Hannah

Hannah was overwhelmed and she simply had no words. Was

this even real? There was her father, standing right in front of her. Finally, after years of wonder and hope, he was actually here. She had found him.

Her father looked at her with warmth and curiosity. He pulled up a chair and sat down. "This is so bizarre," he said, but he looked at her with a smile and she tried to smile back. She was frozen stiff. She simply couldn't believe it was actually happening. "*This can't be real*," she had thought it to herself but it came out in a whisper.

"So this is bizarre for you too then, huh?" he was looking straight at her, but not in an intimidating way. It was like he wanted to know what she was thinking, how she was feeling. It was a little daunting. "I've thought about you my whole life. And now you're here," she put her hands on the table, not knowing what to do or how to act. What was he thinking?

"I'm sorry it wasn't sooner. I didn't know."

 They sat in silence for a moment, taking each other in. Hannah looked at his features and tried to find the similarities. The eyes were obvious, but they also had the same nose and the same left dimple.

"So, you live in Surry Hills?" was the first question she asked.

"Yeah, I do. I've been to Melbourne a few times since I moved up there. It has nothing on Sydney though, but then, there's no place like home."

"I hope not," she said without really thinking. He looked at her with concern, but he didn't probe her. Instead he moved the conversation to Sydney.

"Have you been to Sydney? I could show you one day… I mean… if you want to. That's probably a bit forward. I'm sorry."

He was talking too fast and he was clearly nervous. Somehow, his nerves calmed her and she smiled at him.

"Yeah, I think I'd like that. You'd have to show my sister too though, she'd be super jealous."

"Oh is that so, you have a sister?"

The conversation started to flow and Hannah became more and

more at ease. Her butterflies lifted as her father spoke to her, keen to make conversation. She allowed her mind to drift, to contemplate a new life. He seemed interested in her and her life. He was warm and friendly and everything she could have dreamed of. She blinked back tears, but this time they were tears of joy. For the first time, she felt a sense of hope, a hope with direction, with purpose. She was experiencing the feeling of genuine happiness for the first time and it felt unbelievably good. Was her life finally about to turn around?

She felt like she could sense the change...

Printed by Amazon Italia Logistica S.r.l.
Torrazza Piemonte (TO), Italy

13496776R00112